KING ARTHUR'S
Ransom

TALES · OUT · OF · TIME

KING ARTHUR'S
Ransom

DONNA VANN

Tales out of Time

King Arthur's Ransom
Copyright © 2003 Donna Reid Vann

ISBN: I-85792-849-0
Published by Christian Focus Publications Ltd
Geanies House, Fearn, Tain, Ross-shire,
IV20 ITW, Scotland

www.christianfocus.com
email: info@christianfocus.com

Cover design: Alister Macinnes
Cover Illustration: Neil Reed

Printed and bound in Great Britian by
Cox and Wyman, Reading.

Dedicated to my parents,
with love and gratitude:

Don Reid Jr.
Frances Hawkes Reid

Contents

The King is Dying

King Uther is dying.
I will do anything to make sure
Arthur rules Caerleon after him!

Metal struck metal with a crash that sent birds flying from the treetops in panic.

'One for me!' shouted Arthur as his sword thumped Cai's ribs. A cheer went up from some of the warriors standing nearby. The rest just stood with their arms crossed, watching silently.

I glared at them. I hadn't realised how many supporters Taran had. Arthur will be king when his father dies, if all goes well. But Taran is the strongest warlord. The Council could choose him to lead the kingdom, if they wanted.

Cai leaped to one side, raised the long sword and connected with Arthur's shoulder. Arthur staggered and the birds scattered again.

'My point!' Cai grinned in triumph. As Arthur's cousin, he tried twice as hard to win. Though small he was quick on his feet, except when he tripped himself up.

'Careful!' I called to Arthur, ignoring the warrior's sniggers. I knew the swords were blunted but they could still wound, even with padded tunics and fish-scale armour.

Arthur thrust neatly past Cai's shield and knocked him flat on his back in the dirt.

'Arthur, good!' Bem shouted.

I smiled at Bem, who was perched next to me

on the stone wall by the field. He was born with a weakness all down his right side, which gives him a lopsided look. No one thinks about it, he's simply cheerful singing Bem, who's always right in the middle of everything.

I clapped wildly and others joined in as Cai jumped up, ready to fight again.

'Time for lessons, Arthur!'

'Ooo, better go Arthur,' jeered a warrior. 'Can't keep your *little sister* waiting.'

'No, no,' Bem chided the warriors.

'It's all right, I'm used to it.'

I jumped down from the wall and busied myself scratching the ears of Stinker, the huge shaggy brown mongrel who never left Bem's side. He'll eat anything smaller than a barrel, which makes him have farts so strong you can almost see them. He licked my hand and let one out now. I moved quickly aside, joining Arthur who was leaving the training field.

People think it's odd the king's son treats me like a sister. I can't say why, it just happened. My father was a warlord, one of the strongest and bravest men among all the tribes of Caerleon. After he was killed in battle three years ago, my mother shut herself away in the Abbey on the High Hill. I can go and see her any time I want, but she never leaves the compound. I think there's a rule that the nuns and monks must stay there.

'I didn't mark the hour,' Arthur said, pushing his blond hair off his forehead.

A servant darted forward to slip the heavy armour and padding over his head. Underneath, his simple belted tunic showed how slender he was. Thin, almost. As usual his tunic was dirty and fraying at the edges. I thought if he dressed more like a king's son the people would respect him, but he always said respect had to be earned, not snatched at greedily by wearing fine clothes.

'I won!' Cai shouted.

He threw his sword in the dirt and turned a cartwheel. He forgot about the weight of his armour and overbalanced, landing flat on his back. The men broke out laughing and Cai's dark face turned as red as a painted vase. He obviously had the wind knocked out of him and made a few feeble swimming motions like a tortoise turned on its shell. Arthur and I couldn't help giggling.

'You did not win! Arthur clearly beat you!' I added for his ears alone, 'You need to make every win count, let the men see your skill.'

'You worry too much, Little Sister. That was just for fun. When we train properly we use wooden swords; they're twice as heavy.'

'I'm not really 'little' any more, you know!'

Arthur grinned at me. Until this year he was a head taller but I was catching up with him, even though he's a year older than me, almost fifteen. He never tries to make the warriors stop teasing me about being his sister or wearing tunic and trousers all the time instead of the long skirts of a woman. I guess he knows I can take care of myself!

Cai got to his feet and sulked along behind us as we walked down the hill past the war-house, a whole complex of buildings where the warriors lived and trained and stored their weapons.

'You didn't see the whole thing,' Arthur added. 'We were counting points. Cai had ten to my seven, but tomorrow it's my turn.'

I was wasting my breath, as usual.

'We'll sit for a while with Magnus to keep him happy,' he said, 'then I want you to meet us at our place on the High Hill. There's something I have to show you.'

'All right—what is it?' I noticed how serious he looked all of a sudden.

'Later!'

'You're practising with the wooden sword as well, aren't you?'

'Of course!'

'In battle, everything will depend on your skill.'

'An hour each day, without fail. I can kill a man any day with a bit of oak!' Arthur grinned and his eyes sparkled. They looked almost green now, but they changed with his mood.

He simply wouldn't take it seriously. The whole warrior training was an amusing game to him, and to Cai. Why couldn't they understand that Arthur's future, and even that of Caerleon kingdom, depended on him being a better warrior than anyone else? I'd never thought the Council would pick Taran over the king's own son, but now I was starting to wonder.

The villa below us shimmered in the hot summer sun. It was a large square of rooms around a central courtyard, with buildings such as stables and sheds for carpenter and blacksmith outside the square. The river Usk flowed between the king's villa and the town of Caerleon, where the Second Legion had been quartered years ago. After the Romans left, some of their buildings were dismantled and the stones carried across to build the villa compound and wall around it.

'Come on, hurry up, we're late for our lesson!' The boys were dragging their feet as we entered the courtyard by the small east gate and crossed to Magnus' room.

'Greetings, pupils!'

Magnus stood in the door of his work-room, his smile making the lines in his face look even deeper. He was the king's advisor, easily the cleverest man in the whole of Caerleon kingdom.

'You are late. Dare I ask why?'

'We were at training.'

'And you, Vibiana? Are you also training to be a warrior?'

'She's our keeper,' Cai said. 'We'd never get anywhere on time if we didn't have her to boss us!'

I crossed my eyes at him when Magnus wasn't looking and we followed him into the room, a combination of sleeping chamber, study and science laboratory.

Magnus tries his best to keep Roman language and customs alive, which is why he lets me join in the lessons, even though I'm only a servant girl. The Romans left over a hundred years ago and I reckon in another hundred we'll have forgotten all about them, but not if Magnus has his way.

We worked hard for the rest of the morning but I hardly felt tired, unless I looked at the exhausted faces of Cai and Arthur. I held out my wax tablet and glanced up at Magnus.

'Good?'

'Good, Vibiana,' he said with a smile. 'You progress every day. Boys, take note! You will have to work hard to keep up with her.'

Arthur sighed and pushed the hair off of his sweaty forehead. Cai was bending over his tablet, his tongue sticking in his cheek and his dark hair nearly touching the wooden frame. I felt a bit sorry for them; they didn't think learning to read and write Latin was fun, the way I did.

'Have you begun your record-book?' Magnus asked me.

'Yes. I work on it at night when your mother sleeps.'

Magnus had told me write down what happens to me each day, or things I'm thinking about, to practice writing in Latin. He gave me some thin sheets of wood and a quill and sooty ink. I'm hiding the sheets in the chest where I keep my winter cloak. Not that anyone will want to read it. My mother doesn't care what I do; she just sits all day in her cell at the Abbey, praying.

'It's hard work!' I added.

'Your hand will accustom to forming the letters.'

'I mean, it's hard to think what to say. I want to write important things, not just *Today I brushed my hair.*'

'For you, that would be an event!'

I scowled at him and untied the string I use to keep my unruly hair out of my face, then tied it again more tightly. He was one to talk! His hair was like dark earth strewn with snow, and stood out in every direction.

'Now tell me: what is the vocative of *Brutus*?'

'*Brute*.'

'Good! Arthur, it's your turn....'

The lesson continued. After another hour I looked up from my tablet and gazed out the window. From this room at the front of the villa there was a view all the way down to the river and the ruined Roman theatre beyond. Suddenly I realised all the shadows were short and thought of Magnus' mother.

'I must go! Your mother needs me to wheel her out of the sunshine.'

Magnus sighed and nodded. 'Just think, I had hopes of making a scholar out of you!' He frowned, making the lines in his face look like furrows of a ploughed field.

I looked closely and saw his eyes sparkle.

'Go on then! I'll have to make do with these two.'

I heard Cai and Arthur stifling groans as I ran from the room, dodging bottles and jars heaped everywhere on the tile floor.

I never can quite figure Magnus out. He's a bit mysterious and I sometimes wonder what he gets up to when the rest of us are asleep. Especially, what he does with the huge globe of green glass which hangs suspended by heavy ropes over his work bench. I've asked him about it more than once, but he never gives a direct answer.

Sure enough, Zea was sound asleep in the hot sun. I felt guilty. I'm Zea's personal maid now, and her welfare is my responsibility. I had left her in the shade of the largest apple tree, one of many fruit trees which

15

border the beds of dog-roses and vegetables in the centre of the courtyard. It was where we usually sat in the mornings, while she told me stories from her childhood or from the Scriptures. Arthur used to join us most days, but he's grown out of that now.

Zea was old, the oldest person I'd ever known and not even as strong as a sparrow. Magnus had made her a rolling chair out of an old wicker war chariot stuffed with cushions, but of course she could not wheel herself. She depended on me to do it.

Now here she was, baking in the noon heat. I moved behind the chair to grab the handles and she woke with a start.

'Oh! Vibiana, it's you.' She peered up at me and smiled. I touched the enamel clip which held her grey hair in a knot, and scorched my hand.

'You'll catch fire!' I exclaimed, wheeling her across the yard towards her room on the other side of the court. 'Summer should be over, but the days are still hot. You should rest.'

'I already have. No, come and sit with me a while, and I will tell you my dream.'

This was a game we often played, to see who had the best dream. Zea usually won. Most nights I slept like a stone, so I didn't dream.

I guided the chair into the doorway of her chamber and across the bright tiled floor to her usual place by the window. From there she could look out on all the comings and goings in the vast courtyard which was the heart of the villa compound. There wasn't much that escaped Zea's eye! I was thinking I should apologise for leaving her to roast in the sun when she smiled up at me, her face wrinkling like a dried walnut.

'You did no harm. My old bones need the heat.'

'Grandmother, you always read my mind.' I smiled, settling down on the cushioned couch next to her. Of course she wasn't really my grandmother, though sometimes I wished she was.

The light went from her face. 'I had a dream that troubled me greatly.'

Something made my heart squeeze tight. Zea rarely had bad dreams. She always said she was so close to Heaven, it filled her thoughts even at night.

'It concerns you both. You and Arthur.'

17

A Bad Dream

Grown-ups have no sense! Why did we have to wait days and days to learn about the lost torc and the challenge?

I waited patiently for Zea to collect her thoughts. I knew she was simply thinking out the best words. Her mind was clear, and she often saw things with her heart the rest of us missed.

'It was just now, when I dozed in the sunshine,' she began. 'At first it was as many of my dreams these days: I am walking, fit and with two good legs, up a sunny hillside. The light has a golden shimmer, a resonance we do not see on this earth. On each side are flowers I have never seen before, of pure clear colours which sparkle in the brightness. Up ahead I see you and Arthur, climbing high in the meadow.'

She paused and her lips trembled. I moved close to her and took her hand.

'Then a cloud moves across the sun. Not just a dark cloud, but thick with blackness, somehow evil. The cloud descends from the sky, moving towards you. I begin to run, faster and faster, but I cannot reach you in time. The black force envelops you first, then Arthur as well...'

She clasped my hand tightly. I saw tears form in the corners of her eyes.

'What does it mean, Grandmother?'

'I should not have told you. Hear me child, a

dream may mean nothing. Usually our dreams are only cast-offs of the thoughts, like a snake shedding its old skin. I was wrong to worry you with it.' She shifted in her chair, causing the wicker to creak.

'Perhaps I will sleep after all, Vibiana.'

I wheeled her over to the chamber behind the woven curtain, helped her into her bed. As I pulled the soft woollen coverlet up to her chin, she smiled at me. 'Always remember, God goes with us and will guide us through whatever comes, if we ask him to.'

I said goodbye and left her to join Cai and Arthur at the High Hill, above the Abbey. From ancient times people had worshipped their gods in the wood there, but we never went into the wood. It was dark and mysterious, filled with echoes of the old ways. They say the Druids sacrificed children there long ago, and that severed heads of their victims once hung in the trees.

I climbed the hill to our meeting point, an outcropping of rock just below the wood. I couldn't put Zea's dream out of my mind. It wasn't the dream which upset me, but the way she reacted to it. She was usually so strong! What could it mean, this sudden weakness the dream left her with?

Although I loved hearing Zea tell Scripture stories, I felt uneasy when she talked to me about God. I don't know why; of course I was a believer, like everyone. But she seemed to have a faith that was stronger than anything I ever felt.

Cai and Arthur were waiting for me on top of

the flat rock. Cai stood up and waved. Arthur was seated, holding what looked like a scrap of parchment in his hand. I thought he looked worried, which was quite unlike him.

'Finally!' Cai said. 'How long can it take, to wheel an old woman across a courtyard?'

'I had to do something else.' I'd tell Arthur the dream later, when Cai wasn't around.

'What's that?'

Arthur held out the parchment. I sat next to him and took it from his hand. It was stained with age and the markings were faded. The sketch showed a neck-ring such as warriors wore, a circlet of metal like a twisted snake.

'A torc. Your father wore one into battle, when he was –' I stopped short of saying, when he was healthy and led our warriors well.

'Yes, but not this one. Look closely.'

I peered at the drawing and saw that the rounded ends which would clasp around the throat, were formed into some kind of animal. 'Dragons?'

Arthur nodded. 'The symbol of our people. I found this parchment in my father's chamber last night, when I sat by his bed. Someone had left it on his table. I thought I had heard of it.'

'Go on, tell her! You are the slowest storyteller I know!'

'It's the golden torc of our legends,' Arthur said.

'Oh yes, the ruler wears it to battle, and victory is assured. It's been lost for ages, according to the old tales.'

'Maybe it's more than a tale.' Arthur heaved a sigh and leaned back against a boulder. 'I showed this to my mother, and you won't guess what she told me. There was a meeting of the Council, and they decided whoever could find the torc would rule after my father's death.'

'What are you talking about?'

'Who will be king.'

'You will, of course!'

'That's what I thought. But now my step-sister has come up with this wild idea about finding the torc.'

Morcanta! I could just picture it: the woman with her long flame-red hair worn in the old style, parted in the centre and bound by a cord around her forehead. She'd lecture the Council of Elders in that haughty way of hers, and they'd do whatever she asked.

She had taken over the running of the villa several months ago, once the king became so ill that the queen refused to leave his bedside. I'd had several encounters with her. It was clear she didn't think a servant girl should be treated like a friend by Prince Arthur.

'Can you believe it?' Cai was fuming. 'The Council met days ago, and no one even bothered to let Arthur know!'

'I'm sure my mother would have mentioned it, but you know my father's been much worse lately.'

I nodded. Even from outside in the courtyard I sometimes heard the king coughing harshly in his upstairs chamber.

'What did your mother think about it?'

'She told them I was a good warrior already, even if I'm barely fifteen. I don't think they believed her. Taran said the torc was just an old tale. Of course, he wants the kingdom for himself.'

'The whole thing is ridiculous!' I said. 'Even if the old stories are true, there's no way to find a neck-ring that's been lost for hundreds of years.'

'The point is,' Cai said impatiently, 'guess who was the person just before Arthur, to sit by the king's bedside?'

'Uh, I don't know – Morcanta?'

'Clever girl!' Arthur said.

'You think she left the drawing there?'

'I'm sure of it.'

'But why?'

'Why do you think!' Cai said. 'She wants to find the torc so she can rule the kingdom herself. Maybe she's found it already!'

Arthur nodded. 'That could be why she brought up the idea. I've never thought much about ruling the people – I guess I just figured it would happen one day in the distant future. But the idea that my step-sister might grab power for herself –'

I leaped to my feet. 'Arthur, you can't allow that! You have to stop her! The future of our people is at stake!'

'Cai, run get a bucket of cold water to throw over Vibiana!' He laughed. 'Calm down, Little Sister! At least you cheer me up, that's something.'

'It's nothing to laugh about, as far as I can see! Come on, both of you!'

'Where?' asked Cai.

'We've got to start looking for the torc!'

'If Morcanta's already found it –'

I shook my head. 'No, don't you see? Why would she bring the drawing to the king's bedside? She wanted to ask him if he knew where it was.'

'But he's too ill to answer,' said Arthur. 'Besides, he would have told me before now, he would never have kept such a thing secret. So maybe you're right, she doesn't have it.'

'If you're worried about anyone, it ought to be Taran,' said Cai.

'Why? Except that he hates Arthur and would drown him in the river, if he could get away with it! Is he looking for the torc?'

'He doesn't need the torc. All he needs are plenty of warriors who don't think a boy should rule them. Then he could easily overpower Morcanta.'

Arthur frowned. 'Both of you have to face the truth: Taran is a much better warrior than I am. He's stronger, more experienced –'

I shook my head to clear it and turned my back on them. All my life I had believed, not merely believed but *known* as surely as I knew my name, that Arthur would be king some day. I felt my safe, secure world was about to be shattered. Did the black cloud of evil from Zea's dream warn of this?

My eye was caught by something moving up the valley. It was a horseman, riding swiftly. As he came closer I recognised the horse, and then the rider. No one else had a steed of that glossy midnight black. No other warrior had such a long dark moustache. I pointed and the three of us watched as Taran circled the Abbey compound and rode up the hill towards us.

The Blow of a Sword

It took the blow of a sword
— the thought of losing a sword—
to shock Arthur out of his laziness.

Arthur jumped up and stood flanked by Cai and myself, as Taran reined in his mount.

'Greetings, Arthur.'

'Greetings, Taran. What news?'

'I reckon you know already.' A large man on a large horse, he looked down at Arthur with a scornful expression, ignoring Cai and myself completely.

'State your business plainly!' I burst out.

Arthur made a shushing motion with his hand. Taran didn't even glance at me. If I was a warrior, I'd show him a thing or two! I blew my breath out through my nose and managed to hold my tongue.

'Perhaps you will explain what you mean,' Arthur said politely.

Taran inclined his head. 'The Council met with your mother, to consult about who should rule – after your father dies.' I saw Arthur stiffen at this. I guess I'm used to my father dying, but it was still to come for him.

'Naturally she has you in mind. But you're only a young pup, after all – you haven't even fought in one battle!

'Your step-sister Morcanta wants the kingdom for herself. She gave us a challenge: whoever can find the lost ancient torc, will be seen to be chosen by the gods.' He grinned as if he found this a huge joke.

'This is nothing new.' Arthur lifted his chin, looking Taran straight in the eye. 'It's a foolish idea. Any kitchen servant who found the torc would be king!'

'The Council would never allow that. It's understood it must be a warrior, but your step-sister fancies herself in that role. Perhaps she intends melting down all her gold bracelets to make a torc!'

Taran dismounted, leaving his horse to graze. I couldn't help feeling like a cat with a large dog invading its space. His muscular bare arms were tattooed with swirling designs.

I dug my fingernails into my palms to keep from blurting out something rude. Cai scowled and shifted from one foot to the other, but Arthur seemed calm.

'You did not climb the hill just to tell me this,' Arthur said.

As he stood there, tall and fair in the sunshine, I thought what a truly good king he would be, and knew I would do anything to make sure that happened.

'No, you're right. Here's the thing.' Taran smoothed his long moustaches with one hand. 'You're a sensible lad. Surely you see you're not ready for this. Just say the word, I'll step in for you. Let you have time to grow up, train, find your feet. As soon as you're able, I'll move aside, seeing as how you're the rightful the king and heir.'

'Wouldn't you like that!' I shouted. Arthur shot out his arm to keep me from lunging at Taran.

25

'Hush, Vibiana. Taran, it's a reasonable request.'

Taran shrugged. 'I reckon when you do think about it you'll say no, so here's another idea. Man to man, you and I both know this tale of the torc is just an old story to keep people entertained around the fireside. We can settle this in the traditional way.'

'You mean single combat?'

'The two of us, hand to hand in a fair fight.'

'But it wouldn't be fair, would it! Arthur will be twice the warrior you are, but he must grow into it!' I paused, realising I had insulted my friend without meaning to.

'Thank you, Little Sister,' Arthur said with a faint smile.

'I just want –'

'– the best for me. I know. Taran, I will think on this. What of the Council?'

'They don't want Morcanta. And they figure we could be waiting ages for someone to find the torc. I reckon I can persuade them that we'd get a quicker result this way. Of course, I'll give you plenty of time to train.'

Arthur nodded, but his eyes were cold as a winter's morning. 'That may be what we don't have. Time. My father ill, rumours of invaders beyond the river. I will think on it,' he repeated.

Taran inclined his head and turned away to make clucking noises for his horse. In a moment he was trotting back down the hill.

'I don't believe him!' I said as soon as Taran was out of hearing.

'Nor I. *Of course, I'll move aside*' Cai mimicked. 'He's determined to get rid of you, one way or another

– he'll either kill you in combat or let you die of old age waiting for him to give you the kingdom.' He kicked at a stone and stubbed his toe hard.

'He's right, you know,' Arthur said.

'About what?' I asked, ignoring Cai who was hopping around yelping like a hurt dog.

'He would be the better ruler. I simply don't have the experience to lead men into battle. And I can't see myself beating Taran in single combat, except by a miracle.' He settled down again against the boulder, tugging irritably on a hunk of blond hair that flopped over his forehead.

Cai and I both stared at each other, stunned.

'You're giving up?' Cai asked.

I thought of something else. 'What would your mother say?'

Arthur looked sheepish. 'I know. No one would understand, she least of all. But shouldn't I do whatever is best for the people?'

'Pig-slop!' I shouted. 'You as king, that's what's best for the people. We could at least try to find the torc.'

Arthur grinned at me. 'All right, I'll agree to that at least. Where do we start?'

'Well,' I said, thinking fast. 'We could ask Magnus what he knows. If anyone can find lost ancient objects, it will be him!'

'Agreed.' Arthur clambered to his feet.

'Any ideas on where it might be?' Cai asked Arthur as we headed down the hill.

'Who knows?'

'We should gather together every possibility, then explore them one by one,' I said.

27

'That would take forever,' said Cai.

'Not if we don't have many ideas,' Arthur said. 'As for me, I can't think of a single one.'

I was silent, letting my eyes travel over the scene below us: the Abbey compound, where men and women quietly tilled gardens or prayed; below that, the walled villa with its chambers and outbuildings; beyond the villa, Caerleon town and the ruins of the Roman amphitheatre.

'It could be lots of places! For instance, buried under one of the stones in the old theatre.'

'Oh good idea,' said Cai. 'How many years would it take us to dig up every stone in the place?'

'Well if you've got a better idea, say so!'

'Calm down you two,' Arthur said. 'Vibiana, there's only one problem.'

'What's that?'

'During the time when the torc supposedly went missing, the Romans were here and the amphitheatre was in use. I can't see anyone burying our sacred treasure in the centre of Roman activity.'

'I guess you're right.' I felt deflated.

'What about somewhere in the Abbey enclosure?' Cai said. 'Maybe they buried it under the altar in the chapel.'

'The Abbey wouldn't have been here either.'

'No,' Arthur said. 'Face the truth: the torc was stolen by someone passing through. Now it's probably in the treasure house of the emperor of China!'

We found Magnus in his work-room, seated at the table next to Gruffin, the red-cheeked servant boy who worked for him. They were peering into a large bound book. I didn't know Magnus was teaching Gruffin to read Latin, but I guess he figured the more Latin readers the better.

'What are you reading?' I asked.

Magnus looked up and slammed the book shut. I got a glimpse before he closed it and it didn't look like Latin after all. Gruffin jumped up and scurried to the other side of the room where he grabbed a broom and began to sweep the stone floor like a whirlwind.

'Just an old book of wisdom, handed down to me by my mother. It is worth a great deal, so I keep it locked up.'

Magnus flicked a glance at Gruffin, who darted forward and snatched the book, locking it up in the tall cupboard where Magnus kept all his valuable books and scrolls. He had been collecting the written word for years. According to him, learning would vanish one day if someone didn't work to preserve it.

'So, the three of you want more lessons?' Magnus spoke heartily, standing and walking towards us. It was odd, but I had the feeling he was trying to distract us from thinking about the book. Which, of course, meant I definitely would think about it. Arthur handed Magnus the bit of parchment with the drawing of the torc. Gruffin stopped sweeping and tiptoed closer to see.

'Ah. So your mother has told you. I had hoped she wouldn't worry you just yet –'

'She didn't tell me until yesterday when I found this by my father's bedside. I think Morcanta left it there.'

'Where did the drawing come from?' I asked. 'How did Morcanta get it?'

'I gave it to her,' Magnus replied. 'It has been in my safekeeping for years. I thought, with the king near death – I am sorry Arthur, but we must face the truth – it would be good if the torc could be found.'

'So it was your idea! But if Morcanta finds it, she'll take the kingdom!'

'Now Vibiana, calm yourself. I have no doubt the three of you can outwit Morcanta. I would not have suggested it otherwise.'

'Just now Taran has come with a different challenge,' Arthur said.

'He wants to fight Arthur in single combat!' I said. 'That's not fair, is it Magnus? What are we going to do about it?'

'That's for Arthur to say, I think.'

'Well,' said Arthur, looking away from Magnus, ' actually I've been thinking it might be best for the people if we all just agree that Taran is the most capable ruler for now. He says it would only be until I am ready to take over.'

'Oh, he does, does he?' Magnus pursed his lips.

'But first we're going to see if we can find the torc,' Cai said.

Arthur frowned. 'We have so little time. I don't know how long – even if we take a few weeks, what is that? It's been lost for centuries.'

'My mother would suggest you pray,' Magnus said.

'Don't you pray?' I asked. The whole villa gathered each morning and evening in the chapel, for prayers and psalms. Now that I thought of it, I didn't often see Magnus there.

He shrugged. 'I have never seen the point of worshipping a God who is so weak, he would come to earth as a human and die.' He smiled at us to take the sting out of his words.

'Well, we've got to do something!' Cai said.

'If not praying, then what?' I asked.

'There may be other avenues.'

I waited for Magnus to explain that, but he didn't.

'Conceding to Taran sounds like a reasonable plan,' Magnus went on. 'He is an excellent warrior. Giving him the kingship would increase his natural powers. Even those who now oppose him might eventually give in, and our people would be united under a strong leader.'

I couldn't believe what I was hearing! I was about to interrupt when I saw Magnus twitch one bushy eyebrow at me in warning. Arthur stared at Magnus, his face suddenly flushed.

'So you agree.' Arthur heaved a sigh but for a moment his eyes had a lost expression.

'Why not? It seems expedient. Of course, there is one thing you may not have considered.'

'What is that?'

'Caliburn.'

'My father's sword?'

'It will pass from your father, not to you as his son and heir, but to Taran as the ruler of the people.'

Arthur's mouth dropped open and his eyes blazed. He drew himself up and spat out one word: 'Never!'

He turned and strode from the room, fury in every line of his body.

Cai hurried after him and I moved to join them, when I felt something tug on my tunic. Gruffin leaned forward and spoke softly, not letting go his grip.

'Magnus can find things. You could ask Magnus.'

As I pulled myself free and ran after Cai, I glanced back to see the wise man standing quietly in the shadows. It was too dark to see his expression.

Who Will be Third?

*Maybe now the warriors will stop
teasing me and calling me
'Little Sister'!*

When I caught up with Arthur, his fists were still clenched. If he'd had Caliburn with him just then, I think he would have swung it at someone.

When he saw me he relaxed slightly. 'Caliburn was the sword of my great-grandfather,' he said. 'My father says it was forged in a secret place deep underground, helped by the god of war. My mother doesn't like to hear him talk of the old gods, but he told me once when we were out hunting boar.'

'It's a wonderful sword!' Cai exclaimed, making huge swirls with his right arm in the air.

'How would you know?' I said. 'You probably couldn't even lift it!'

'Just give me a chance!'

Arthur shook his head. 'Caliburn is special. My father has never let me so much as touch it. He won dozens of battles with it, and now—'

'It hangs on the wall in his chamber, waiting for you!' I was hoping to distract him from his gloomy thoughts.

'Becoming king isn't something I can refuse just because I don't feel prepared. I can't deny who I am. I must find Caradoc!' He headed for the war-house with Cai on his heels.

I followed more slowly, thinking about Magnus

and what Gruffin said. Maybe I should thank
Magnus for giving Arthur a sharp nudge by
reminding him about Caliburn. The man was a
puzzle to me. I knew he served the king loyally and
wanted Arthur to rule.

Could Magnus really find the torc? Then why
hadn't he done that already? I determined right then
to get him alone, without Gruffin, and ask him what
this was all about.

Crossing the courtyard, I passed under the
windows of King Uther's chamber and heard a
racking cough ring out, long and tortured. I knew
he sometimes sat in the upstairs atrium in the fresh
air, away from the sight of all except the nurse and
his family. You could hear him coughing from
anywhere in the court. People were starting to
whisper that it wouldn't be long now.

I glimpsed Morcanta at the door of the kitchen,
giving orders to one of the servant girls. At first I
wanted to avoid her, but then I thought, why should
I always have to look out for her? Let her do the
looking out for a change! I deliberately walked that
way so she'd be sure to see me.

Morcanta glanced up as I passed, and I stared
back, greeting her in my most cheerful tone.

'Good day, Morcanta!'

Arthur's step-sister tossed her head and her hair
gleamed red-gold in the sun. She was beautiful,
though it was beauty that didn't reach into her heart,
assuming she had one!

'Servants do not address their mistress in that
familiar way,' she replied in her cool voice. Her pale
face seemed washed of colour in the bright sun.

'True, Morcanta, but you're not my mistress.'

The kitchen girl's eyes bulged.

'You think not? Ah well, things change. You serve a mistress who is old and weak. You have a privileged place because of her, and because my step-brother Arthur is a bit stupid. Zea will die soon, then where will you be?'

I was furious. She managed to insult both of my favourite people at the same time! I opened my mouth for a rude reply, but just in time I saw the corners of her mouth turn up. That would make her happy, if I said something so bad she could have me punished.

'In any case, you don't do enough work to earn your keep. When *I* am ruler of Caerleon –'

I turned and ran, not trusting myself to say anything at all, I was that angry. I ran all the way to the war-house, where I jumped up and down on a pile of straw in the yard until I felt calmer and bits of straw were scattered everywhere.

What was it about Morcanta and me? She wasn't pleasant to anyone, but to me she was always downright spiteful. She was right in a way: as Arthur's friend and Zea's maid, I had little work and a favourable position. Maybe she was jealous.

A stone trough for washing stood by the doorway to the armoury, so I dunked my face and gave it a good splashing to cool off. It wouldn't help to come all flustered to this important meeting with Caradoc. I wondered what he would say about the lost torc and above all the challenge from Taran.

Inside the armoury Caradoc was pointing to swords and daggers of various sizes hanging on the wall. Arthur and Cai were nodding. Evidently I had missed the whole thing. I slipped up and joined them quietly.

To be honest, I was in awe of Caradoc. He was short and stocky, not a person you'd notice in a crowd. But you'd be wrong to ignore him. He knew every trick of battle ever used from the ancients to the Romans, plus some no one had thought of. He could toss the lance or spear farther than anyone else, was expert at thrusting the short Roman sword, but was just as skilled with the long double-edged sword.

More importantly, he was a natural teacher. If Caradoc taught you, you learned and remembered. For some time now he had been instructing me in use of the short bow, while the boys practised with swords. He said if I kept it up, I'd be able to take on the best of his archers one day.

I trusted Caradoc. He was loyal to King Uther through and through.

'Vibiana.'

I waited but that was all. Caradoc was a man of few words.

'Good day, Caradoc.'

'Caradoc says he can train Arthur to beat Taran!' Cai said.

Arthur nodded eagerly. His whole attitude had changed. He seemed to believe it would be possible, and I reckoned if Caradoc believed it, that was enough for me.

'When do you start?'

'Today. Right now.' Arthur grinned at me and rolled up and down on his toes. I thought I had never seen him so excited about anything. Then all of a sudden something flashed through my mind, a picture of Arthur lying wounded, bleeding, Taran standing over him ready to plunge in his sword one last time. I gasped and opened my mouth but no words came out.

Caradoc squinted at me but the boys didn't notice, they were so busy taking down the swords one at a time, feeling the weight of them, being careful not to touch the sharpened blades.

I felt a bit dizzy but I shook my head and the picture faded. It must be the heat, I thought.

'We need a third,' Caradoc said.

'A third what?' asked Cai, leaping well back to swing a heavy sword nearly as tall as he was.

Caradoc held up one hand with a stern look. Obviously he knew Cai's reputation for clumsiness. Cai sighed and replaced the weapon carefully on its hooks.

'Training partner,' said Arthur, running his hand over the swirled design on the handle of the sword he was holding. 'Caradoc says if I train with two people coming at me, it will be that much easier when there is only one.'

'Who will be the third?' I asked.

There was a short silence, then they all three turned and stared at me.

It's Not Easy With Family

It is easy to talk with friends,
to make them understand. Sometimes I wish
it was not so hard with your own family.

'Me?' I stammered, my voice high and squeaky with disbelief.

'Why not?' Arthur replied, laughing out loud.

I frowned, wondering why that was so amusing.

'She's only a girl!'

That settled it.

'I'll do it!' I said, looking daggers at Cai.

Caradoc stared at me thoughtfully for a moment, and I squirmed but stared back.

'I may be a girl, but I'm more quick on my feet than they are!'

Caradoc nodded, then his mouth creased in one of his rare smiles. 'You'll do.'

'One thing,' he added. 'You must ask your mother.'

'What!' I stamped my foot in frustration. 'I don't have a mother.'

'Yes you do. Ask her.'

Which was why I was now trudging slowly up the High Hill to the Abbey enclosure. I could have run it easily, but I wasn't in the mood. I hadn't seen Llian in months, nor did I want to. I realised I didn't even call her 'Mother' any more in my thoughts. She was like someone I used to know once who had died or gone away.

How would I begin? How long would it take me to get to the point, that the only reason I was coming to see her was to get permission to practice being a warrior? What would she say— Llian, who had turned her back on the world and its warriors and lived a life of complete peace and serenity?

The compound was vast, including broad patches of vegetables as well as grazing and stabling for cows and goats, all behind a long woven wattle fence. Chickens pecked and scratched in the dirt, doing their best to stay out of the way of huge pigs which sauntered freely in the open spaces. In spite of the pigs it all looked clean and orderly.

Except for the small stone chapel, the buildings were low thatched structures of wattle and daub: two separate long sleeping huts for men and women, a smaller round one, plus some sheds and outbuildings. I was glad to see the nuns and monks working outside, for I dreaded arriving and finding them all in the chapel, or even worse, in their separate cells at prayer.

'Vibiana!' A woman called to me from a patch of leeks. Was that Llian? They all looked alike in their plain belted robes. No, this woman had dark hair, and Llian's was straw-coloured, like mine.

'Your mother is in the cowshed.'

I nodded my thanks and entered through the front gate, looking around until I spotted a large thatched open shed at the rear of the enclosure. As I moved to the entrance the sour smell of damp straw hit me. In the dim light I saw the backs of two robed figures. One was kneeling and the other stretched out prone on the ground. Were they praying even in the cowshed? I was mortified.

Just as I was about to tiptoe away a loud bellow pierced the air.

'Here it comes!' called one woman.

'Pull!' yelled the other.

The next thing I knew, there was a tremendous clamour, like a giant caught in a trap. The women were shouting and wrestling with something, then they both gave a cry. I crept forward until I was right behind them. The air was thick with bits of straw and dust and the heat of the struggle. A huge brown cow lay there panting heavily, eyes closed. I saw a little calf lying on the dirty straw. Its eyes were open but didn't blink. I held my breath, but the calf didn't move.

'Is it dead?' I whispered. They ignored me.

The kneeling one did something to the calf's mouth. It twitched and began to suck in air. Then the woman got to her feet and lifted the calf, placing it on the straw at its mother's head. After a moment the cow seemed to notice the calf and she opened her eyes. She lifted her head and sniffed the creature, then stuck out her rough tongue and began to lick. As she licked the calf from head to toe, it came awake and finally began struggling to sit up.

'Well done, Llian!' murmured the woman who had carried the calf. She returned to kneel on the straw next to Llian and the two women spoke a brief prayer of thanks.

Llian sat up, a look of delight on her blood-streaked face. The front of her undyed robe was filthy from lying face down at the back end of a cow, but she didn't seem to mind. Then she noticed me and her mouth flew open.

'I've never seen a calf birthed,' I said, more to cover my confusion than anything else.

'Llian is our best midwife.' The woman smiled gently at me. 'I'll go clean up,' she added, and slipped out of the shed. I was alone with the mother I scarcely knew.

She jumped to her feet and rubbed her dripping hands on the front of her robe. Then she shook her head and ran over to a large earthen bowl of water and dipped and washed them as best she could. Finally she turned to face me.

'Vibiana,' she said, trying to smile. The middle of her forehead puckered.

I'd forgotten about that. It was a sure sign she was worried about something, probably me. I suddenly got a brief but clear picture of my parents. I was walking between them holding their hands, gazing up at them as they laughed and chatted together. I felt tears start to my eyes and I was annoyed. I never cry! I hoped Llian hadn't noticed. I stared down at my feet.

'I am so glad you came to see me.'

This was making it harder for me.

'Uh, well.'

'I hear news of you,' she went on. 'Every day a servant comes up from the kitchen to get vegetables from us, and I ask about you.'

'It's true,' she said, smiling at the look on my face. 'I hear about your lessons with Magnus, and how good you are with Zea. I know you are happy there, as I am here.'

'I'm not always happy.' Something about what she said bothered me. I saw the wrinkle appear again on Llian's forehead so I plunged on.

'The reason I'm here is to ask if you will grant permission for something.'

Disappointment flickered across her face, but she nodded. I explained about Arthur's challenge, and wasn't too surprised that she'd already heard all about it. The kitchen was the best place in the whole of Caerleon villa for gossip.

'So the thing is, Caradoc says Arthur needs a third training partner. And, well, they've asked me.'

Llian nodded. 'You've always been quick on your feet. Is it dangerous?'

'Not very, or Caradoc wouldn't have suggested it. I'll wear padding and we'll mostly use wooden swords.'

'Then, why not? I will pray for Arthur. If God has chosen him to be king, he will help him be ready for the challenge. He could even lead him to find the torc.'

'Thank you— M- Mother.' It was hard to get that word out.

Llian moved forward as if to hug me, but something in my look stopped her and she let her hands fall to her side. 'Come with me to meet Abbess Brangwen. She will give you a blessing for this new adventure.'

'Maybe another time. I must go now!' I left as quickly as I could, almost running, not looking over my shoulder. I could feel her standing there, staring after me.

The Mystery of Magnus

*Magnus is like a mystery which beckons
me to solve it. I will think it out
and write down my questions.*

'Cai, Vibiana— attack!'

Arthur raised his wooden shield and sword.

I tensed, then lunged forward, waving my
sword. The heavy padded jacket I wore threw me
off balance and I nearly fell on my own weapon.

'Not so wild!' Caradoc cautioned. 'Think! Focus!
Where are you aiming?'

'At his ribs!' I staggered upright, slicing with my
blade, but Arthur was far too quick. With one twist
of his wrist my weapon went flying, and he turned
to counter Cai's attack as if swatting a wasp. I ran
clumsily for my sword but by the time I got it Cai
was clutching his wrist where an ugly bruise was
forming. Arthur tossed his sword into the dirt and
ran to help.

'I'm really sorry! Let me see it.'

'You don't say sorry to the enemy!' Caradoc said.
'Press your advantage!'

But Arthur shook his head and turned Cai's wrist
gently back and forth before he was satisfied nothing
was broken.

Caradoc clucked impatiently. 'You'll never make
a warrior that way! You fight well lad, but what do
we do about your soft heart?' It was as much as I'd
ever heard him say in one go. 'Enough for today!'

We'd been practising with Caradoc every day for the last two weeks. Swords of every size and description, daggers, even wrestling – though I didn't join in that. Sometimes Caradoc swatted Cai and me out of the way and fought Arthur himself. Both boys had to run and vault over wooden horses, weighted down with their full kit. Arthur was good and getting better all the time, but still I saw that he only beat Caradoc because the trainer wasn't using his full strength. Taran wouldn't be so generous, I was sure!

Then there was the wrestling. Cai and Arthur, stripped to the waist, learning from Caradoc how and where to grip your opponent, how to wrong-foot him, leave him lying dazed in the dirt. I didn't know why Caradoc included that in the training, but I didn't question it. He knew best.

Each day I could tell Arthur was a bit stronger, a bit less exhausted by the end. At first he learned to react more quickly; by the second week he was learning to think ahead, to guess what Cai and I might do before we thought of it ourselves. Too bad he couldn't have trained with Taran himself!

Later that day after we cleaned up, the three of us joined Magnus for our lessons. He had let us have a break until now, but said we would forget years of work if we left it too long. We sat on a bench at one side of the long table. It was cool and dark in the room, making the field of barley outside the tall windows look golden yellow. The river beyond was like a skein of silver yarn. Magnus paced up and down behind us, firing questions: 'How do you say *it is made* in Latin?'

'*Fit.*'

'Cai, well done! Quickly, the gerund of *eo!*'

'Ah –'

'Try again, you know this: the locative of *Londinium.*'

'*Londinii.*'

'Excellent, Vibiana!'

This went on until my whole head felt numb. Cai dug his fingers into his short dark hair, sweating more than he had at the training ground. Arthur frowned.

'Magnus – a question.'

'Of course.'

'Is this any use? What good will it ever do me?'

'That depends on what you mean by "good". I could say that learning is *good* in and of itself, that it expands the mind, helps one be able to think and reason. A question from me – who gave you your mind?'

'God, of course.'

'Does God want you – all three of you – to make good use of his gifts?'

Arthur smiled. 'I understand. Learning is to the mind as a warrior's training is to the body. It will help make me ready for the challenges to come. Fair enough. But we can already speak enough Latin to get by. Why do we have to learn the grammar?'

'These days with so many people from other countries right here in Caerleon, you need Latin even to buy a length of cloth at the market. It is the one language common to all. But I hope someday you will be able to do more with it than conduct trade.'

Magnus sighed, and his dark eyes lost their fire. 'I

fear a day is coming when all this –' he waved his hand towards the locked cabinets of books and scrolls lining the walls – 'will be swept away. People will lose the art of reading, even the books themselves may be lost. Centuries of learning – gone!

'Perhaps, who can tell, one of you three might help to keep learning alive. To do that, you must know how to read and write it correctly. And of course, if you want to read the Scriptures, Latin is essential.'

'Why don't you give us the Scriptures to read?' I asked. 'We know the stories already, that would make the reading easier.'

I glanced to my right, to the worktable in the corner and the green globe. I remembered seeing Gruffin lock away the strange old book he and Magnus were looking at, in the lower cabinet behind the table.

'I do not possess the Scriptures,' Magnus said in reply to my question. 'Perhaps that would be a good addition to my library. I must look into it.'

'What about that book from your mother?' I blurted out. I really wanted to ask him about the globe, but that came out instead.

'It is not the Scriptures! Now, on to science: who can tell me how Archimedes discovered the king's crown was not made of real gold?'

Arthur and Cai both sat up straighter and started talking at once. I quickly got bored and stared around at the room, chewing on the end of my stylus. Magnus always gave me the same one, because I kept putting it in my mouth without thinking.

My eyes wandered as they often did to the huge globe of green glass, bigger than my arms could reach round. It hung over the worktable, with a tall fat candle behind it. If the candle was lit, the flame would shine through the centre of the glass. I'd never seen it lit and was just about to ask Magnus if he would light it.

'Gruffin!' Magnus said suddenly. 'Bring me some fresh sand from the storehouse.'

'Yes, Master,' the boy replied. He'd been sitting in the shadows humming to himself, but he quickly scooped up a bucket from beneath the work bench and left the room.

'You use a lot of sand, don't you?' I said, distracted from the candle.

He nodded. 'Many of my experiments involve the use of fire, and I always keep a special fine sand in case things go wrong.'

'Why sand?' Cai asked.

'Think!' Magnus commanded.

'Because,' Arthur said, 'pouring sand on a fire smothers it.'

'Yes, but why?'

The three of us stared at him blankly. Magnus smiled and waved his hand gently back and forth.

'What does the fire need, to live?'

I could only guess, from the motion of his hand. 'Air?'

'Vibiana, my star pupil!' he exclaimed. Arthur grinned at me and Cai rolled his eyes.

'I didn't know, but I saw what you were doing with your hand...'

'And you took a leap sideways with your mind,

came up with the right answer! At least, the answer my experiments have told me. When the fire has no air, it goes out. That is why a candle placed inside a beaker will scarcely burn. The flame must be able to breathe.

'Enough for today,' he continued. 'And will you two boys please learn to imitate Vibiana, and use your intellect?'

We returned our waxed tablets to their place on a shelf and went out into the dazzling sunshine. The boys immediately started punching each other and running around. They didn't much like sitting still for so long, and had to balance it out with action. Normally I would have joined in but today I simply shuffled along behind them, scraping my sandals on the hard dirt. My heart felt full of doubts concerning Magnus but I couldn't think out clearly what my questions were.

Too Soon

*It is too soon! I know Arthur
is not ready. From tomorrow,
nothing will be the same.*

'Tell me about your son.'

Zea laughed. 'You have a strange way of talking sometimes, my child!'

It neared evening, and the heat had lessened. We sat by the fountain in the courtyard, Zea in her chair and I on the bench behind her, combing her long hair. Truth to tell, there was less of it now. I remembered only last year it was still thick and glossy, though it had always been grey. Not always of course— Zea said it was once as gold as a coin, and fell to her waist! It was hard to see in this bent old woman the fresh young beauty she sometimes talked about.

'You come right out with a thing, before you think. Perhaps that gets you in trouble, but I like it!' She laughed again, a light chuckle that made her sound young. That made me sad. It reminded me how old she was. Even with the hypocaust it was cold here in winter, and the elderly often died then. No, I would not think about that!

'Ouch!' Zea said. 'Not so roughly, if you please! What do you want to know about Magnus? I'll tell you what I can, though if I'm honest, there is much about him even I don't know or understand.'

'That's how I feel as well. I came in once when he and Gruffin were looking at an old book–'

Zea shook her head and clucked with her tongue. I stopped combing.

'You know it? I thought he was teaching Gruffin to read, but why would he do that? And furthermore, I don't think it was Latin!'

'It's a mystery, that book. And not a nice one, I think.'

I twirled her chair around so I could look into her eyes.

'But he said *you* gave him the book!'

She gasped and her watery blue eyes glazed with sudden tears. She pressed her thin lips tightly together and shook her head again, so that the tears came loose and started slowly down her wrinkled cheeks.

'No,' she said in a low voice. 'I did not. The book came to him from my sister, who was—'

'Never mind, Grandmother!' I patted her hand and wheeled her around again, combing her hair up into a twist and securing it with the enamel clasp. I was furious at myself for causing her distress and hoped she could forget it.

'Let's go and see what Fulvia is preparing for us! Roast lamb, I think.'

I grabbed the handles of her chair and wheeled her across to the kitchens. There wasn't space for us to enter, but the long room was open to the court. Fulvia was short and grey-haired, ruling her domain quietly but with total control. Servants moved gracefully about in the narrow space, each seeming to know exactly what to do without asking. I chatted to Zea about the lamb roasting over the flames of a brick oven, the herbs being furiously pounded in a giant pestle, the leeks bubbling in a vast cauldron.

She nodded dutifully at each bright thing I said, but my heart was heavy as a sack of stones. Why couldn't I watch my tongue? Why did I always have to speak before I thought things out?

Our meal was brought to us in Zea's chamber by a servant, who set the tray on the low table by the sofa. We ate in silence. As usual, everything on her plate was minced small using sharp knives in the kitchen, as she didn't have all her teeth. She watched me eat as she always did, letting her food grow cold enough not to trouble her ageing mouth. I tore into my food with my hands and spoon, remembering to use the finger bowl and towel when needed. I was starving for some reason. Finally, I had eaten every crumb on the table except Zea's unappetising soupy food. I sat back, stifling a burp, and finished off my beaker of ale.

'Are you ready to eat?' I picked up her spoon.

She shook her head. 'I have no hunger.'

'It's because of what I said, isn't it. I wish I could think first!'

Zea smiled weakly. 'But then you wouldn't be Vibiana! Don't change. I love you the way you are. The problem isn't you–' Her voice trailed off.

'Come!' I said brightly, digging the spoon into the brown mess that was the roast lamb. I knew she meant, the problem was her son. I'd wanted to ask her about the green globe as well, but I could never open the subject of Magnus with her again. I'd just have to find out some other way.

'Vibiana.'

I started and looked up. Arthur stood in the doorway. His hair was ruffled and he looked distracted.

'Pardon me, Grandmother,' he added.

'What is it?' I asked.

'When you are finished...'

'Oh, she is finished now,' Zea said, smiling. I'd only managed to give her about five bites, but I knew she wouldn't take any more.

'As you wish, Grandmother,' I said. 'I'll come soon to help you to bed.'

Zea nodded but her thoughts seemed to be elsewhere. Arthur walked silently beside me as I carried Zea's tray back to the kitchen.

'What is it?' I asked finally. 'What's happened?'

'It's tomorrow. The combat.'

'With Taran? Tomorrow! How can it be – you're not, I mean, are you ready?'

Arthur smiled. In the fading light his face looked pale and tired. 'No, I'm not ready— no use pretending, I know it as well as you do! But my father is hovering on the edge of death. His cough –' He shook his head.

I didn't need to ask. It was whispered all over the villa that the king was coughing up blood.

'And I suppose it was your idea to have it tomorrow.'

'Taran's.'

'Humpf!'

'But I agreed to it. If my father dies before the question is settled, there will be chaos.'

'Arthur, have you told her?' Cai burst on us out of nowhere. 'What time? Will you choose the weapons? It's not fair if Taran decides everything! You're best with the old swords, don't you think? Though the Roman ones are quick – you can thrust it into his heart with one blow, *wham*!

'The idea isn't to kill him, cousin.'

'Ha!' I said. 'I bet Taran thinks it is! He'll be out for your blood. If it goes too far he'll say sorry, and rule happily without you around to bother him!'

'We will fight hand to hand,' said Arthur. 'No weapons.'

'No weapons!' Cai and I both shouted.

'No. That was Taran's idea as well. He's not trying to kill me, just win the kingship – and Caliburn.'

Now I understood why Caradoc had spent so much time wrestling with Arthur, showing him different holds and tricks. He must have known this was a possibility. Though Taran was stronger, Arthur might be able to outwit him. At least, that's what I told myself.

And if he didn't? Taran would rule; Caliburn would be his, and the kingdom as well. The last of the light faded into darkness, echoing the gloom in my heart.

An Uncertain Result

I should be glad it was not worse.
Now there is even more
to worry over.

The flat packed earth of the training ground didn't seem a grand enough place for the combat which would decide the future of our people. It was an ordinary practice field, used every day by the warriors quartered here.

Today it was crowded. I guess even the kitchen servants had an hour free. Most of the villa servants were there, and all the warriors. Taran's supporters stood behind him, looking fierce. I almost giggled when I saw them—each and every one wore a long moustache, just like their hero. I hadn't noticed that before, not seeing them all together.

Arthur had his loyal supporters too, the king's true men. They stood silent and still, as if waiting for something which they wished would never come. At least it wasn't raining. That was the only good thing I could think of!

Caradoc stood behind Arthur who was stripped to the waist. He was helping Arthur twist and turn and bend, all to limber him up for the fight. I tried not to think how pale and slender Arthur looked.

Cai was there, and, of course, Bem and Stinker, and I saw Morcanta on the edge of the crowd. Her white face was cold but there was a glitter in her eyes. Strange that she hadn't argued against this conflict which left her out. Next to her was the woman who attended her. She dressed in imitation of Morcanta, with flowing hair bound by a circlet over her forehead, but her face was pock-marked and her nose was curved like the beak of a hawk.

I looked for Queen Aurelia, but couldn't see her. Perhaps she didn't want people staring at her, talking behind her back about what would happen to her if Arthur was beaten.

The crowd chatted in low voices. Suddenly a sound like the whisper of wind in the trees began on the outer edges of the gathered people, grew louder and closer until I could make out the words: 'Taran is come!'

They parted to let the challenger through. He strode towards us, head high, the sun glinting on his sleek dark hair. He wore tartan trousers and his torso was bare. There was something about his skin —

Dismayed, I turned to whisper to Arthur. 'His skin. It's *oiled.*'

Arthur and Cai turned to look. Arthur seemed paler than before – maybe that was just by comparison with Taran, who was tanned with muscles like knotted rope. His skin shone like the scales of a fish and his swirled tattoo made his arms look even thicker.

'That's not fair!' I muttered fiercely.

Caradoc shook his head at me in warning. From a small leather pouch at his side he drew out an earthen flask and uncorked it. I let out a sigh of relief. Arthur's skin would be oiled, as well. I wondered how this would affect the combat and whether Arthur was prepared for it.

Magnus walked to the centre of the circle, and

the crowd went silent. For this occasion he wore an outer robe of royal blue trimmed in gold, looped across his shoulder in the Roman style. Arthur and Taran stepped forward.

'People of Caerleon,' Magnus said, his voice booming loudly, 'you have come today to witness a fair combat between Prince Arthur and Taran, warlord of Caerleon.' He paused briefly and the crowd began to murmur the names of their favourites. I heard Taran's name mentioned more than Arthur's but hoped I was mistaken.

'You'll win, I know you will!' I whispered fiercely at Arthur's back.

'The winner,' Magnus went on, 'will follow King Uther as ruler of Caerleon. As a sign of his sovereignty, he will receive the sword Caliburn.'

At this the noise of the crowd swelled. People were standing on tiptoe, trying to get a glimpse of this ancient weapon, so well known but never seen.

Caradoc stepped forward. He held Caliburn flat in his outstretched palms, lifting it high so the crowd could see. There was a loud 'Ooh!' and some clapped their hands in delight. It was long and sleek, the double-edged blade glinting in the sunlight, designed more for ease of handling than for beauty.

I saw Arthur's shoulders stiffen at the sight of the sword. I knew he would do his best to win, to keep from losing Caliburn and the kingdom. But would his best be enough?

Caradoc moved to one side, placing Caliburn on a large flat boulder near the edge of the field.

In case of a question, the winner would be decided

by Magnus, Caradoc and Rhys, one of Taran's men. The three stood around the edge of the circle, at an equal distance apart from each other.

'Let the combat begin!' Magnus announced.

Taran and Arthur faced off. The warlord braced himself like a sturdy tree planted in the dirt. Arthur looked focused, but seeing him next to Taran made my heart sink into my toes. Good thing Arthur didn't glance my way; I'm sure my fears showed on my face.

There! Arthur lunged first, that was a good sign. Yes, he wrong-footed Taran! *Ahh!* from the crowd. The big man easily righted himself, shaking off Arthur like a pesky horsefly.

He lunged again –

'Arthur, look out!'

Taran tipped him up, turned him upside down over his shoulder and fell backwards on top of him! Arthur crashed to the ground and lay in a daze.

Taran thought he'd won. He leaped to his feet and raised his arms gleefully, not even turning to see if Arthur was hurt. The crowd went wild; I don't think we even knew who we were shouting for. I had my fist in my mouth, willing with all my might for Arthur to stand up.

Oh! Arthur was raising his head, slowly coming to a sitting position.

'Go Arthur! You can do it!' I was jumping up and down, waving my hands in the air.

Arthur waited until Taran was walking past him. Then he shot out his legs to grip the man's legs like a scissors. Yes! He tripped him!

Thok! What was that sound? Taran staggered, fell back heavily. His head hit the dirt with a tremendous thump. He lay still.

Three of Taran's men ran to him, but they didn't touch him, waiting to see what the judges would say. Was it over? Taran wasn't dead, I could see his chest heaving.

Magnus, Caradoc and Rhys put their heads together. Rhys was arguing, I could tell that. He stepped into the circle and picked up a stone from the dirt, taking it back to show Caradoc and Magnus. Where did that come from? Arthur is victor! He must be! I was holding my breath.

Magnus stepped into the centre and raised his hand for silence.

'If anyone saw who threw this stone, you are to tell me.' His dark eyes flashed around at the crowd, but no one spoke.

Taran still lay on his back, but his eyes were open. An angry lump appeared on his forehead. His men tried to help him up, but he shook them off and managed to rise. He stood red-faced, swaying slightly, waiting for Arthur to speak first. Arthur stared at him for a moment, then he quickly moved to the boulder where Caliburn waited. He grasped the hilt with both hands and heaved the sword into the air.

'No – unfair!' Rumbles of discontent rose from the crowd until most people were shouting 'Taran, Taran!'

'Arthur tripped him *before* the stone hit him!' I yelled, but no one listened.

Arthur's clear voice cut through the din.

'Caliburn must wait! It would be wrong to disqualify a brave and excellent warrior through someone's trickery. We'll meet once more, this time next week.'

'Do you accept?' Magnus asked Taran.

Taran drew himself up. I had the feeling he desperately wanted to refuse, that he didn't want to humble himself to accept the offer. There was a moment's dead silence, then he nodded. 'I agree.' He turned on his heel and strode away.

The crowd broke out in exclamations, most of them angry or disappointed. Taran's supporters knew he should have won and Arthur's thought he was a fool to let the chance slip through his grasp. I didn't know what I felt. I glanced at Magnus, who stood a little back from the crowd. He saw my questioning look and smiled at me, giving a slow nod.

Arthur placed Caliburn back on the stone as gently as if the sword was made of fresh eggs.

So Magnus was pleased! I took a deep breath, then went to see to Zea.

Something I Didn't Want to See

I don't like to think of what I saw in Magnus' chamber. Questions can lead to unpleasant places. Yet they must be asked. I have always believed this but now I wonder.

Strange how quickly the year can turn. Next day, the autumn rains began. Before the week was over the river flooded, and any thought of combat had left most people's minds. Not mine, of course, nor Arthur's. Surely not Taran's. A few of us still wondered and worried about the fate of Caerleon.

I woke early that morning to the sound of rain drumming on the tile roof. I pulled back the heavy curtain to see the courtyard already covered with a thin layer of water. The day should have dawned but it was as gloomy as deep twilight.

A damp chill permeated the room. I ran to Zea's bed; her eyes were open and she smiled at me. I touched her cheek and it was cold as ice.

'You're freezing! I'll fetch a warm brick from the kitchen.' I knew it was too early in the year for the hypocaust, but maybe I could persuade someone to start it. It took three servants to get it going and keep it stoked, and I reckoned they'd have more than enough to do with the heavy rain. Ages ago the hypocaust ran all year long, but the western woods were disappearing in the constant demand of the furnace. These days we had hot baths and heated bed chambers only in winter.

Zea nodded but didn't speak. Quickly I grabbed

my own bedding and placed it on top of hers, tucking everything neatly in around her shoulders. Then I rummaged in the chest for a woollen shawl, pulling out my own winter cloak. The growing bundle of my own written 'book' I left securely tied with cord in the bottom of the chest.

I arranged the shawl as best I could around Zea's head.

'Don't move!'

'I don't think I can,' she whispered, with a trace of a twinkle in her eye. 'You have me wrapped like a pudding in a bag.'

'You won't cook! Now try to sleep a little more, and I'll be back as soon as I can.'

Before I left, I lit clay lamps to give the feel of warmth, even though it was false. I pulled on the hooded cloak and found my wooden pattens hiding under a chair. Slipping my bare feet into them, I opened the door and stepped outside. I kept under the columned veranda as long as I could, then darted across the flooded courtyard. Cold water immediately sloshed into my pattens. I might as well have gone barefoot.

With my hood up and eyes squinted against the driving rain, I almost missed seeing the light at one of the long windows of Magnus' room. Good! I would tell him about his mother; perhaps he could order the hypocaust fired up.

I ducked under the veranda on that side of the courtyard. It was still early. I didn't want to shout or knock. Anyway, the door to his room was not shut, though a heavy curtain covered the entrance.

I removed my pattens and slipped into the room barefoot, pushing back my cowl.

'Magnus,' I said softly, then I stopped. He was seated at his worktable with his back turned to me. The hanging glass globe was aglow from the candle flame behind it. Magnus was staring into the glass, his hands stretched out, lightly touching it on either side. He hadn't heard me.

He began to speak and at first I thought he was addressing me. But then I caught the words, only they were words such as I'd never heard. Were they Latin? No, I knew well the clipped sounds of that language. These words flowed into each other like the chuckling of a stream, never stopping. I'm not usually one to hold back, and I had my mouth open to ask him what he was doing, but I didn't. There was an atmosphere in the room, something that made the hairs on my scalp tingle.

I crept back out past the curtain, stepped into my pattens and made my way in the downpour to the kitchen. The servants gladly let me have a warmed brick wrapped in a cloth, and a fresh-baked roll which I ate on the run. Zea was sound asleep when I returned. I placed the cosy bundle carefully under her tiny feet.

By now the day had arrived, looking more like dusk. I crossed again to Magnus' chamber, making a loud noise on the stone walk outside his room with my pattens.

'Magnus!'

In a moment the tutor shoved the curtain aside.

'What is it, eager pupil?' he asked, smiling. 'You are hours too early for your lesson!'

I glanced past him into the room, but the candle was out and the globe was scarcely visible in the dim corner. Quickly I explained about his mother, and his smile turned to a frown. I waited outside while he found his own cloak and wooden shoes, then we went together to Zea. The water in the courtyard was lapping at our heels. If this kept up, Zea wouldn't be the only one ill!

When we entered the chamber, we could hear the rasping sound of her breathing.

'She wasn't making that noise before!'

Magnus stepped to his mother's bedside and put his hand gently on her forehead.

'Go and find Justus! Tell him I want the hypocaust lit immediately. Then fetch Gruffin. He can go into Caerleon town and get the doctor.'

'I can go myself. I can run faster than Gruffin, you know I can!'

Magnus hesitated, then nodded. 'Go quickly! But watch out for the bridge – it may not be safe in this rain.' He pulled up a chair and sat next to Zea, not bothering to remove his cloak.

My pattens were outside the door under the veranda, and I dropped my cloak beside them. They would only slow me down. Not for the first time, I was glad to be wearing trousers! Zea couldn't let go of life now, she just couldn't! I splashed through the courtyard, my whole body tense, willing her to stay alive.

How Long?

*How long will it be? What happens
to a people when two of its strong pillars
are removed? Will Caerleon live on?*

I ran through the gate and down the hill towards
the river. The surging water had not yet swamped
the stone bridge. My tunic and trousers were soaked
now, clinging to my skin. After a while I didn't feel
the cold so much but the pelting rain struck me with
the force of arrows.

Most of the shops were shuttered. The baker
was open and several people jostled together in
the covered space, waiting for bread. One or two
glanced up in surprise as I ran by.

'Vibiana!' It was the doctor's daughter, a girl of
my age.

'Julia! It's Zea – where's your father?'

'At home!'

I nodded my thanks and kept going. A right turn
onto a narrow street, then left, then right again.
Finally! I hammered on the closed door with my
fist.

An upstairs shutter flew back.

'What is it?' shouted the doctor. He always
seemed rude and in a hurry, yet I knew at a patient's
side he was calm and kind.

'Please come quickly, Zea is ill.'

He nodded and snapped the shutter closed. I
didn't wait for him, but raced back the way I had
come. The space of a man's height was left between

the bridge and the rising water. Everything was grey – river, houses, all the land around. I was distracted by thoughts of Zea but vaguely wondered what would happen if the river flowed over its banks, if the bridge gave way.

I heard Zea's tortured breathing as soon as I entered the chamber.

Magnus was still hunched in a chair at her bedside. He looked like he hadn't moved, but his cloak had been laid out on top of the blankets covering his mother's small frame.

'The doctor's coming.'

He nodded.

'And the hypocaust?'

Before he'd said it I was out the door again, looking for Justus who managed the villa estate. I found him in the storehouse, giving orders to servants carrying barrels and sacks up to the loft.

When I explained about the hypocaust he sighed, then nodded.

'I'll see to it. The king will have need of warmth, in any case.'

I thanked him and went to tell Magnus. On the way I met Arthur, who was heading for his father's chamber. He was glad to hear the about the heating.

'I should have thought of that myself! Send the doctor to my father after he's seen Zea,' he said.

I wanted to ask more about his father, and also if he and Taran would still fight. But obviously this wasn't the right time.

At Zea's bedside, the plump doctor seemed worried. 'This salve, three times a day,' he barked at me, handing me a small stoppered pot. 'And these herbs brewed, it's important she keeps drinking. This will wash the poison from her body.'

I gave him Arthur's message. He nodded and left abruptly. Magnus still sat there, his thoughts apparently far away.

'Go, if you want,' I said. 'I'll sit by her.'

'All right.' He took the bag of herbs from me. 'I'll take these to the kitchen for you.'

I changed into dry clothes and curled up in the chair by Zea's bed. All that day I sat next to Zea, listening to rain on the roof. The tiles under my feet grew pleasantly warm, but I kept the oil lamps going to ward off the gloom. A dozen times I bathed her forehead with a cool damp cloth. Three times I rubbed Zea's bony chest with the salve; twice I was able to rouse her to drink a little of the dark smelly brew which a kitchen girl brought over. Magnus came in twice to see how she was.

'No change either way.' But when he stuck his head in the room a third time, I smiled at him.

'Better now, I think.'

He came over and touched her forehead to find, as I had, that it was damp but cool. He gave a huge sigh of relief and his face crinkled into a grin. I was startled to see his eyes were wet.

'She will do very well,' I added, to cover my embarrassment.

After a moment he nodded. 'You are free to go. I will stay the evening.'

The rain had ceased for now and the night air felt freshly washed. I slipped around the veranda, the stones cool on my bare feet after the warmth of the hypocaust. It was time to start wearing the shoes that most of us left off all summer. I didn't look forward to the chilly shorter days, especially not if the rains kept up.

When I came to the king's quarters, my steps slowed. A light burned in the upstairs sleeping chamber. Maybe the king was feeling better. His servants were bringing him food and drink. He wouldn't die after all, and Arthur would have time to grow up, learn his warrior skills before having to take on Taran!

'Vibiana!'

The whisper jolted me out of my reverie and I jumped slightly. Arthur stood in the darkened doorway of the king's quarters.

'Arthur!' I felt guilty, as if I'd been spying on his parents. 'How is your father?'

He shrugged and gave a heavy sigh. 'There are days when he seems so much better, I have hope. But tonight he's as bad as he's ever been.'

'I'm sorry.'

'I know.' He grabbed my arm and pulled me along with him.

'Where are we going?'

'To the kitchen.'

'What for?'

'Food, what else?' He laughed at the look on my face. 'Come on, there's been enough gloom and sadness today. Race you there!'

We hurled headlong across the courtyard, splashing through puddles and getting our clothes thoroughly soaked. Arthur had a head start and won easily, but in spite of that I was smiling by the time we reached the kitchen. It was usually open to the courtyard at this time of year, but curtains had been drawn against the rain. We sat at a wooden table in the corner, snug in the waves of heat from the large brick oven.

'Fulvia, do you have any left-overs?'

'I might, for you.'

The grey-haired cook wiped her hands on her apron and moved to uncover some dishes on a side table. There was rest of a huge meat pie, some pickled onions and half a round of bread. Suddenly I remembered I had not eaten since the night before, except for the roll at breakfast.

Fulvia smiled at our appetites, pouring us full beakers of ale.

'There. The way you're always hungry, it reminds me of your father.'

Arthur grinned back at her. Funny, how some people have known you so long and so well, they can say anything and you never take it the wrong way. Their kindness makes up for all kinds of unpleasant things. I felt that way about Zea. Just by existing, she made my life more bearable.

A hearty 'woof' rang out.

'No wet dogs in here!' Fulvia exclaimed, as Bem stuck his head around the curtain.

He nodded and we could hear him ordering Stinker to stay outside. Bem came inside and took a pickled onion when Fulvia's back was turned, tossing it outside for Stinker. He joined us at the table, and before long Cai came as well.

Bem started singing a song he'd made up, and Fulvia and her servants stopped to listen. His face lit up and I wondered how old he really was. We thought of him as young but he had the kind of innocent open face that could have been twenty or forty.

> *In a dream he stood*
> *by a pond in the ancient wood*
> *where gold gleamed on the ground...*

It was Bem's way to collect words he heard here and there, set them to a tune which he would sing under his breath continually. He could put words together in complex ways as long as he was singing. Zea said it was a special gift: the singing set him free, for he never could speak like that.

Bem sang for us the whole evening, halting every so often at the sound of the dog hawking up onion, out on the veranda.

I should have paid more attention to the words of Bem's first song. But I was caught up in my own thoughts, grateful that the king and Zea still lived, wondering how long they could hold on.

Still Asking Questions

*Arthur has proved himself an excellent leader,
why do others not see it? It was his idea
that saved the villa from flooding.*

We walked slowly along the high bank. Not the
riverbank – that was gone completely. We were on
a grassy ledge east of the villa compound, with a
view to Caerleon town below.

It was mostly a view of water. Instead of a river
there was a vast lake, with trees struggling to get
their heads clear of the surface. The bridge had held
but only the top of its stone arch was visible. The
houses nearest the river had disappeared, and water
lapped at the doors of others. Even the sun peeking
through the grey clouds looked watery.

At least the villa didn't flood, and all because
Arthur had ordered Justus to have channels dug, so
the water coursing down from the High Hill would
drain off. I overheard Justus tell Magnus later that
he hoped Caerleon would have the ruler it deserved.
No one dares say things like that openly, for fear of
trouble if Taran or Morcanta should take over.

Even after so many days there were still things
floating in the water, and I was glad we were not
close enough to see what they were. Several bodies
had been recovered. From what we'd heard, no
more people were missing.

Yesterday when I was taking the boat across to
town, something heavy had bumped the side.

'Dog,' the ferryman had said quickly, and he was

right. It was a large one, floating stiffly on its side, its long brown fur combed sleek by the water.

I'd thought of Stinker, and then of Bem, and for the first time since the rains began I'd felt like crying. Here was someone's dog, an insignificant creature that dozed by the fire and followed its master faithfully each day and maybe got kicked or petted, depending on the master. And now it was dead.

Today, remembering the dead dog I was glad to see Stinker bounding ahead of us, stopping now and again to gobble down a stone or a few twigs. He wasn't sad about dead animals in the flood or worried about the future of Arthur and Caerleon. Bem trotted behind him, humming, while Arthur and Cai walked on either side of me.

We were quiet, for once. I was wondering what happened to dogs after they died. Did they go to an afterlife, like people? If Stinker went to Heaven, would he still eat pickled onion and have smelly farts? What about people? Was there really a wonderful afterlife, waiting for those who believe in the Lord Christ? I knew Zea was convinced of Heaven. She was patiently waiting to step into a place filled with beauty and light and God.

'Why are you sighing?' Arthur asked.

'It sounds so wonderful,' I murmured, then realised he didn't know what I was talking about. 'Heaven, I mean. Is it real? Is that where – Zea will go?'

'And my father.' He paused, staring down at the watery landscape.

'And we all, who believe in Christ,' said Cai. 'But the unbelievers, they will be banished to darkness.'

'Yes, I know the teaching as well as you! But what about – well, Magnus? Is he a believer? He seems to believe many things. What about me?'

'You!' Arthur threw back his head and laughed. It was the first time I'd heard laughter in many days, and it sounded strange.

'What's so funny?'

'You, Vibiana. Of course you are a believer.'

I shrugged. 'I'm not, not really. Not like Zea, or my mother. Or your mother. Or you!'

'You are at chapel with us each morning and evening. You say your prayers.' Arthur was staring at me, his hazel eyes turning almost yellow the way they did when he was thinking hard.

'We all go to chapel and say our prayers. It's expected of us. But –'

'But what?' Arthur stopped and Cai scampered ahead to catch up with Bem.

'What does it mean – inside ourselves?'

Arthur pursed his lips and walked on. 'I'm not sure what you're trying to say.'

I wasn't sure how to explain it, if he didn't understand.

'Have you never questioned it? Wondered if we go to chapel and say our prayers only because our parents taught us to? What if your parents had taught you the old ways, worshipping many gods, sacrificing in the woods...'

'I haven't questioned my belief. I don't know why, it just hasn't happened. Maybe it will. Do you think it would be good for me if I did?' he added with a smile.

'No. But why am I the only one who wonders about things like this?'

I dug the heels of my winter boots into the soft dirt. Even I thought it was too cold now for bare feet.

'Because you're Vibiana! What would we do without you – life would be dull, I'm sure! Race you!'

We sprinted forward, slipping and sliding on the wet grass of the hill. I was the first to reach Bem and Cai, if only by half an arm's length.

'You need to keep training!' I scolded him, as we pulled up short by the others. 'You've been lazy since the floods came. How will you face Taran if you can't even beat a girl in a short race!'

'I know, don't remind me!' He was almost too winded to get the words out and I frowned in disgust. 'Caradoc wants me now, in fact. I must go.'

Arthur said goodbye and strode off towards the war-house.

'Boat on the water!'

I nodded, looking in the direction Bem was pointing. I picked out several rowing boats which went out each day, collecting the dead animals.

'There!' He gestured eastward.

'I don't see anything,' Cai said.

'Nor I.' But I'd never known Bem to be mistaken, so I peered more intently.

I saw it! A mere speck on the distant horizon, where the river flowed down towards the sea. Something – too large to be anything but a boat – bobbed on the water. The three of us watched,

Stinker weaving impatiently in between us, as the boat drew slowly nearer.

'It's got a sail!' Cai said.

'Several people,' I added. They all seemed clothed from head to toe in plain brown.

'People!' Bem agreed. He began to run downhill and we followed, Stinker bounding and barking with joy.

Who were they? Not traders, who always wore the brightest colours possible, to herald their wares. Not warriors – I saw no sign of shields or spears.

I tumbled down the hill, suddenly full of energy, feeling that something unexpected was about to happen.

Travellers

*Nothing in my life up to now has prepared me for
these travellers from across the sea. I want to learn
more about them and why they came to us.*

Stinker reached the landing first, with Bem right
behind. Cai and I followed more slowly, keeping
our eyes on the strange boat. It was a wooden craft
like I'd never seen before, not especially large but
with a curiously curved shape and one sail, with a
large red cross stitched onto it.

'Monks,' I said, understanding now why they
all wore brown.

The wind was light and the boat sailed slowly
upriver. I wondered if they were for us or Caerleon
town, but soon it was clear they would dock on
our side of the flooded river. As they drew near, I
saw they were all men.

'Why are they bald?' Cai asked.

'I don't know. Do you think they're from some
country where all the men look like that?' Monks
shaved a circle on the top of their heads, I knew
that, but I'd never seen anything like those smooth
high foreheads.

'No, look, they're shaven!'

Cai was right; I could see now each of the dozen
or so men was cleanly shaven from ear to ear, but
the rest of their hair hung behind to their shoulders.

'One's a boy!' I saw a youth about my age, also
wearing a brown hooded robe. He was not shaven
but had curly dark hair which fell below his ears.

The boy saw me staring and smiled, raising a hand in greeting. I raised my hand in reply, and then Cai caught on and waved at the boy, shouting 'Welcome! Welcome to Caerleon!'

The ferryman caught their line and secured them to the dock. The tall monk who stood in the bow was first ashore. He stepped onto the wooden dock with slow dignity. A large leather box hung by a strap across his chest. In spite of his grey hair his face was scarcely lined and his blue eyes were clear and piercing. I was sure he was the leader; I saw the way the others showed him deference, waited in the boat to see what he would do.

Bem smiled at the monk, who seemed to be expecting something to happen.

'Go on,' I whispered to Cai. 'Someone has to give them greetings in the king's name.'

Cai looked around quickly as if hoping to see Arthur right behind him, but only a few servants were about. They'd stopped whatever they were doing and were simply gawping at the robed monks and the graceful boat. I whispered to a servant girl standing nearby she should warn the Abbey of visitors. She dropped her basket of eels and made off at a run.

Squaring his shoulders, Cai stepped forward.

'Greetings, travellers,' he said to the leader in the Latin tongue. 'Welcome in the name of King Uther of Caerleon. I am Caius Aurelius, nephew to the king.'

'Greetings,' the monk replied. 'I am Feoras.' He had a voice deep as a well, full and round, suitable to his broad shoulders, a voice made for giving orders or

perhaps for chanting songs. Then just as I'd thought
that, he began to recite a poem:

> *We come from green Erin,*
> *you made us welcome.*
> *We bless you in the sacred name*
> *of the Triune God.*
> *We bless you and your house,*
> *your cattle and your dear ones.*
> *The light of Christ will shine upon you,*
> *for often He comes in the stranger's guise.*

I wondered if the monk had made this up on
the spot. Cai's eyes were huge and he obviously
didn't know what to reply to a poem, so he simply
gave a deep bow. This seemed to be the right thing,
and the monk inclined his head, then beckoned to
his followers to join him.

One by one, the robed men stepped from the
boat. Some were young, some old; some were
round, others thin as fence posts; some laughed and
chatted in a strange language while a few gazed
solemnly into the distance, as if they could already
see Heaven.

Last of all came the boy, leaping easily over the
side. He had something tucked under one arm and I
moved closer to see what it was. He saw me looking
and laughed, then angled the object across his chest
and moved his hand across it.

Of course – a harp! It was slightly smaller than
the ones our people liked to play at feasts, and
decorated with the symbol of a woven cord in bright
colours. The boy plucked the strings and began to

sing a haunting song in his own tongue. All of us stood quietly to listen. I'd never heard anything like it.

The music ceased and there was a moment of silence to savour its beauty. I quickly wiped the hem of my sleeve across my eyes and walked over to the boy.

'Welcome,' I said in Latin. Now I was very glad of Magnus' skill as a teacher. 'I am Vibiana.'

'And I am Brendan.' The boy seemed eager to talk with me, even though his Latin sounded awkward and the accent was strange. 'We come from the island of Hibernia, have you heard of it? Our Abbot knows the Abbess here. Are you in the household of the king? Are you a follower of Christ?'

I couldn't help laughing at his many questions, thrown out quickly in his stumbling Latin.

'Yes, I have heard of Hibernia, but I have not met anyone from there. I am a servant in the king's household, but also a friend of the king's son.' I didn't know how to answer his last question.

'And, you are a follower of Christ?' He peered more closely at me and smiled.

I hesitated, then said, 'Yes, we are all Christians here.' That was true, and perhaps this young monk from Hibernia would accept it and not ask more prying questions.

Cai and Abbot Feoras led the way up to the villa gates. The monks followed, then a few of our servants carrying their meagre possessions, which included sacks of grain and casks of ale. I walked next to Brendan at the rear of the procession.

'So, you are a monk?'

Travellers

'Not yet!' Brendan said. 'My parents have sent me to live at an Abbey near our home in the West, to try out my vocation. Maybe I will join the community. Or who knows, I might be a travelling poet!' He strummed his harp and began to sing a rousing song with a beat like that of feet marching up a hill. We all quickened our pace. It made a simple act of walking seem like a glad adventure.

I was almost skipping to the music when we neared the villa gates. Then I stopped. Standing in the open gateway was a woman of middle age, dressed head to toe in white linen. Her cowl covered her hair and a band of white linen crossed her forehead. She waited, tall and solemn, for the monks to approach. Abbess Brangwen!

Abbot Feoras approached and bowed. The Abbess inclined her head.

'Welcome, travellers from Hibernia,' she said. 'The peace of Christ be with you.'

'And also with you,' replied the monks.

This formal greeting over, the Abbot reached forward, took both the Abbess' hands in his large ones, leaned forward and gave her a resounding kiss on both cheeks. All the monks broke out in smiles, and the Abbess didn't seem startled.

Soon all had entered the villa courtyard, where they were welcomed by Morcanta. I guess Arthur was still with Caradoc, and Morcanta seemed to feel she was in complete charge now. Not for long, if I had my way!

Morcanta led the monks into the long dining room to sit and take refreshment before going up the hill to the Abbey. I wheeled Zea over from her quarters to join the excitement. She was so much better now, almost like her old self, though even more pale than before. If she could just last the winter!

We sat on comfortable cushions on benches in the warm dining room. The kitchen produced a full meal: stuffed olives and snails, roast pigeon and lamb, fish boiled in a sauce, honey cakes and grapes for dessert. There was plenty of beer, and I was surprised the monks could enjoy themselves so much. I guessed it was a rare treat for them, instead of their normal fare of bread and cheese.

Brendan ate little. While the rest were feasting, he leaned back on his cushion and played and sang lively songs that the Hibernia monks found amusing. The singing attracted others from the villa, and the party kept growing. Arthur showed up after a while, and also Magnus. Taran was there too, with some of his warlords.

I leaned on the arm of Zea's chair, full and happy, listening to Brendan's cheerful music while I glanced around the lamp-lit room. There was Magnus, deep in conversation with Abbot Feoras, and Morcanta snapping her fingers fiercely at the head servant. Taran was laughing loudly at some rude joke.

Bem sat leaning against the wall behind Morcanta, singing his own words to Brendan's tune. I couldn't hear what they were, but once I noticed Morcanta turn to stare at him.

They were all here, except for the residents of the Abbey compound. Arthur, seated near Magnus, gazed vaguely around as he ate quietly. How I wished all of Caerleon could be united under the hand of that fair and just king I knew Arthur would be! If he could only beat Taran – or find the torc.

The golden torc! With Zea's illness and the flood I had almost forgotten it. Did it exist? Where was it? Some comment floated to the top of my mind – 'there are other ways to find the torc' – who had said that?

I remembered then, it was Magnus. I stared hard at the wise man, wishing I could read his secrets. He was listening intently to something Feoras was murmuring in his ear. His deeply lined face gave away nothing.

Morcanta's Schemes

Morcanta is carrying out some deep plan of her own. She reminds me of a beautiful red spider, quietly spinning a dangerous web.

For weeks Bem had been singing his song about the gold found in the wood, the tune becoming more and more complex but the verses essentially the same. His continual singing was part of the background of our lives. I never thought about the words as a message.

Foolish me! It wasn't until I saw Morcanta in a hooded green woollen cloak slip through the mist, following Bem and Stinker up the High Hill. Then the meaning of these words I'd been hearing for days suddenly flashed like a lightning bolt in my mind. Had Bem wandered into the wood and found the ancient neck-ring? True or not, I was suddenly sure that was what Morcanta thought.

It was just two days after the monks from Hibernia arrived. They would stay several weeks, it was said. I wondered what they would do here. I had decided to go and find Brendan, see if he would come down to the villa and sing for us. I was very curious about a boy of my age who would leave his home and sail across the seas with a group of men in brown robes.

That was when I saw Morcanta trailing Bem. I changed direction, keeping close to trees along the way, skirting along the fence bounding the Abbey vegetable fields. In spite of his awkward rolling walk,

Bem moved quickly. Stinker bounded alongside, looking like a small brown pony in the distance. Morcanta was about a hundred paces behind. Once she stopped, flicked back her hood and turned to stare behind her. I darted behind an oak and held my breath for twenty heartbeats, touching my face to the rough damp bark. Had she felt my eyes upon her? When I dared to peep round, both Bem and Morcanta had disappeared.

Where was Arthur? I looked carefully in all directions behind me, but I knew he was holding vigil at the bedside of his father. Even Cai would do! Where was he?

'Vibiana!' I turned, startled, to see Llian waving at me over the wattle fence. She was in the middle of a leek bed, a hoe in her hand.

I ran to the fence, my thoughts in turmoil. When there's no time for thought, you have to act from your heart.

'Llian, I need your help!' I blurted. I didn't have time to think about the startled look on her face, or to slow down and be more polite.

'Please, send someone right now to find Arthur. I think he is with the king. I have to go into Druid's Wood, but I need him to come!'

Llian nodded, her eyes wide. 'I saw Morcanta following Bem. What's wrong?'

'Can't explain – I'll tell you later!' I was already halfway up the hill at a gallop when I caught myself and turned to shout a thank-you, but Llian was gone. I was right: I could trust Llian! I guess sometimes your heart knows more than your head.

Then I realised I had called her 'Llian' instead of 'Mother' and I blushed in shame. Surely she'd noticed but at least she hadn't said anything.

When I reached the edge of the wood, I stopped to catch my breath. No, that is not completely true. I also said a prayer. Well, what could it hurt? The ancient trees seemed to frown at me and lean more tightly together. I asked the Lord God to protect me and to help me find Bem. As I stepped under the dark canopy I felt the weight of old secrets, horrible things done centuries ago, still locked up in this place.

There is no path into Druid Wood, for no one goes there now. The Druids were the ruling priests of our ancestors. They still practised when the Romans governed us, but in secret. I had heard they took power again after the Romans left, but King Uther put a stop to that. He had declared all Caerleon should be Christian, at least that was the official line. Were there still secret Druids in Caerleon? I'd never thought about it but it was possible.

The undergrowth was dense with vines and brambles, but there was a sort of natural pathway where the growth was thin, and I followed that. Before long I was completely enclosed by tall trees. Many leaves had fallen, but the forest was shady with evergreens such as fir and holly. It was almost like being underground. I was gazing upwards, wondering why it was so dark, when my heart thudded in my chest. In the oaks overhead clumps of dusky green clung to the branches. Mistletoe!

I must be near the exact spot where Druids had worshipped. I knew mistletoe was sacred to them.

Now that I had time to think, I regretted my headlong dash into the wood. I'd seen no sign of Morcanta or Bem, wasn't sure I could find my way out again.

A low moan made me jump, until I heard it again. Only some forest bird. That reminded me there were other creatures here, even wild boar, large and extremely dangerous. And wolves! I had forgotten that. I picked my way forward as quietly as I could, my senses alert for any movement. I broke a branch here and there from a low shrub as I went along, so I could at least make my way back to this spot.

Something rustled stealthily in the bushes to my left. I stood as still as I could, forcing myself to breathe slowly and quietly. The rustling stopped. My heartbeats sounded like war drums in my ears. I waited for ages, but no sound came. I had no choice but to go on.

Then I heard the murmur of voices up ahead. I crept forward until I could see Morcanta standing with Bem on the edge of what looked like a circular clearing. At least, the trees were less dense overhead. I was making my way slowly along when I stumbled into something hard. I put my hand out and carefully pulled back some prickly vines, feeling springy moss and rough stone. It was some kind of object made out of stone, about half my height and twice that in width, flat on top.

'Dearest Bem, come with me!' Morcanta's voice was silky-soft. 'I will give you honeycakes and a new woollen tunic. You can sit by my fire, sing me your songs.'

I had to swallow my spit to keep from laughing out loud at that. Morcanta, the charmer! What a joke!

'Fine lady.' Oh Zeus, it looked like Bem was blushing! Surely he wouldn't be taken in by her! I tried to rush forward, but ended up caught in a vine and fell face-down among the brambles.

'Ouch!' I struggled to my feet. 'Bem, don't listen to her. She's trying to trap you!'

Morcanta's melting expression froze solid. 'You!'

Bem looked from me to her, his kind, open face covered in bewilderment. Morcanta tried to make herself look winsome again, but even though her mouth was smiling her eyes were blazing.

'Dear Bem, Vibiana does not always know what is best for everybody, even though she thinks she does! What can it hurt, to get out of the cold and wet and rest by the fire? I am lonely sometimes, and want someone to sing to me.'

I felt like gagging. 'Bem, come with me instead! We'll find Arthur and Cai, I'll let you play swords with us!'

Bem wasn't listening to me. His gaze was caught and held by Morcanta, whose eyes had now become soft and starry. She held out her hand and he reached for it.

At that moment there was a loud crashing in the brush behind us as Stinker bounded up, a huge dead branch gripped in his mouth. He leaped excitedly towards Bem to show it to him. One end of the branch caught Morcanta and pushed her backwards. She gave a shriek and completely disappeared!

Let Down Again!

*The one person I should
be able to trust
has let me down again!*

'Lady!' Bem shouted.

'Morcanta!' I yelled.

Stinker dropped the branch and barked with all his might. Bem and I started forward but suddenly my feet began to slide. I grabbed his arm and tugged, just managing to keep both of us from slipping over the edge. Now I could tell we were not in a flat clearing, but on the rim of a broad hole in the earth. It was so filled with bushes and small trees it was invisible.

'Help me out!' Morcanta's voice was muffled by the undergrowth but she didn't sound injured, just angry.

'Wait!' I didn't want to end up down there with her. I grabbed the long branch Stinker had dropped, poked it gently downwards through the brush. Morcanta's pale face peered up at me. She lay on her back, trapped in the clutches of a bramble bush.

'Hold on– we'll pull you up.'

Once I felt her weight on the end of the branch, I nodded to Bem. We pulled with all our might and Stinker helped by barking like a mad dog. It took several tries. The brambles didn't want to give up their prize! A couple of times Morcanta lost her hold and slid back into the hole. I could hear her cursing and I'm sure at least once I heard her whimper.

Finally, when she was close enough, we each grabbed an arm and yanked with all our might. She lay face down at our feet, completely winded. Her cloak had come off in the struggle and was left in the hole. Her once fine dress of purple wool was ripped in several places, and her face was covered with scratches. Her left cheek bled freely.

'Are you all right?'

She glared up at me, but I wasn't gloating. It wasn't a nice thing to happen, even to my enemy. She nodded sulkily.

'Bem take Lady home.'

I sighed. 'All right.' What could it hurt? Just because Bem sang about finding gold, didn't mean he had. Anyway, he wouldn't be able to tell Morcanta what he knew. She'd have to figure it out from his songs.

Bem helped her gently from the ground. Morcanta gave a haughty sniff and quickly wiped away a tear, leaving a streak of muck. At first she tried to walk on her own, but she crumpled to the ground and we had to heave her up again. Finally she gave in and leaned on him. They made their way out of the forest, both limping. I followed, and Stinker brought up the rear. He tried to go in front of me, but I blocked him. I had no desire to trail a farting dog through a dense wood! Bem seemed to know the way, and I was glad to let someone else figure it out.

When we reached the edge of the trees it was like coming back into another world. I stepped forward into the misty meadow and felt light, free. There was a feeling of something dark back there that was more than just the close-knit trees. What was that broad hole? Was the large flat stone some kind of ancient altar? What had been sacrificed on it? I shivered, then raised my face to the grey skies and whispered a thank-you that we were all safely out of Druid Wood.

When I lowered my head again I saw a slim figure in brown wool climbing up the hill towards us. When she got closer I saw it was Llian and waved. She waved back, passing Bem and Morcanta with a curious look.

'Vibiana,' she said in a low voice when she reached me, 'I tried to get Arthur but I could not. I sent word but he could not leave his father. He must be very ill; we will pray all night for him tonight.'

'It doesn't matter now. Thank you for trying.'

She peered closely at me. 'I prayed for you in the wood. It's an evil place.'

'I know. I hope I never have to go there again!' I didn't tell her about the altar. Maybe I would later. 'I didn't know you ever left the Abbey,' I added.

Llian looked taken aback. 'I- I don't very often. But I can. We are under no rule to stay inside our compound, but – '

'Never mind. I shouldn't have said that.'

'No, why not? You are my daughter...'

'All this time I thought you were bound by a rule, never to leave the Abbey. But you're telling me it was your *choice*...' I glanced at Llian and saw tears in her eyes. Why was *she* crying? I should be the one bawling my eyes out, because my mother couldn't even bother to come down the hill and see me!

She parted from me without a word as we neared the Abbey. I flounced off down the hill in a temper. I was furious but sorry as usual that I'd spoken my mind so freely.

When I reached the villa, the first person I saw was Cai. His face was grim.

'It's tomorrow. This time nothing will stop it.'

I didn't have to ask what he meant. I simply nodded, and went in to Zea.

*

As soon as I could leave her, I slipped out. The courtyard was dark and chill mist clung to me like cobwebs. I crossed over to Magnus' quarters, shook my head to clear it of the rain and the feeling my head was stuffed with straw. I hesitated – this was something I should discuss with Arthur and Cai. But then I thought of all Arthur faced: his father, the combat tomorrow, losing Caliburn and the kingdom. No! I could not accept that. If there was something else to be done, I would do it.

It was time to ask blunt questions about the book and globe and the wise man's secret arts. I stepped to the doorway and called out for Magnus.

The Book of Ancient Arts

My curiosity is still not satisfied.
I want to know more, yet when I think
of what I might discover, I am afraid.

'Come in, Vibiana!'

The room reeked of hot potions and charcoal.

'Wait. I must watch to get the moment exactly right – there!'

A liquid bubbled in a glass beaker suspended over a brazier. Magnus added a few drops of something from a flask and the liquid turned blue and frothed up. He grabbed a cloth and lifted the beaker from the flame. I watched silently as he held it up, swirling it around. The dim lights of clay lamps gave the scene a mysterious look. I noticed the large candle behind the green glass globe wasn't lit.

'Your candle would give you more light for working.'

'Ah.' Magnus smiled at me, set the beaker down and stoppered it with a wooden plug. 'Did you come to ask me about the candle?'

'Yes, I did.'

'I thought as much. I've seen you staring at the globe. You must learn to keep your thoughts out of your face!'

He motioned for me to sit at the school table, settled himself on the bench opposite. I glanced around expecting to see Gruffin in the shadows.

'Gruffin sleeps in the kitchen. He prefers the warmth, and I prefer some time alone.'

'What do you do with the globe?'

'Do you know how to be subtle? No, I thought not. Never mind, it is one thing I like about you. It does present a problem, though. I expect anything I tell you will shoot straight back to Arthur.'

'But Arthur will be king! He should know what goes on in his own household.'

I blurted this out without thinking, but the look on Magnus' face reminded me. Tomorrow's trial might end it all.

'Besides, he's my best friend.'

Magnus leaned forward. In the lamplight, the lines on his face made him look like a carving out of wood, something old and slightly evil.

'All right. Listen carefully. To do good, we must use every power at our disposal.' He seemed to expect an answer to this but I didn't understand, so I waited for him to explain.

'Arthur wouldn't like what I am about to tell you. Nor would his father and mother, nor my mother, nor your mother. So for their sake, keep this to yourself.'

The hairs raised up on the back of my neck and for some reason I thought of the stone in Druid Wood.

The wise man cleared his throat as if getting rid of an unpleasant taste, and continued. 'When our people became Christians most of them turned their backs on the old ways. They did not want to worship trees or sacrifice to gods in the wood any longer. I agree with that. But why should we also throw out centuries of wisdom?'

Magnus paused, reached inside the leather pouch that hung from his belt, and withdrew a key. He went over to the locked cabinet, opened it and took out the old book I'd seen before. Bringing it over to the table, he plunked it down between us and opened it. A strange smell rose up, probably because it was made of sheepskin and had been shut up in a cabinet.

'I told you this book was from my mother. That was not true, and I regret it. I want to be truthful, even though it is sometimes wiser not to tell all the truth you know.'

'Where did you get it? What's that writing in it?'

'From my aunt, my mother's sister. She was open to the influence of all the spirits, seeing everything that came from the unseen world as good. Some called her a witch, others a wise woman. She travelled to the East and learned magical arts there. When she returned, she brought with her this book, and the glass globe. Years later, she passed them on to me – as well as the knowledge of how to use them.'

Magnus paused, peering at me closely to see how I was taking all this.

'You look a bit pale. Shall I get you something to drink? I have my own jug of wine, I can warm some for us.'

'Yes, please,' I said, more to give myself time to take this in than because I was thirsty.

Magnus jumped up and bustled about like a kitchen servant, finding clean clay goblets for the wine, pouring from a jug into a small pot, setting the pot over the brazier and dipping his finger in it until he judged it warm enough, removing it from the fire and pouring it a bit clumsily into the goblets.

While he did this my thoughts were whirling. Why was he telling me this? Was there something he wanted me to do?

We sipped the warm wine for a few moments in silence.

'I can help Arthur,' Magnus said finally.

'How?'

'I already have.'

My mouth dropped open. 'You told someone to throw that stone?'

'No! I was as surprised as you about that, although I felt sure that Taran would not win. I have an idea about who the culprit was.'

'Morcanta!'

Magnus merely smiled. 'Or one of her allies. Yet Morcanta may have been influenced, without realising it, by certain steps that I took.'

'What were they?'

'I will not tell you in detail, but this book gives instruction in ancient arts. I am able, sometimes, to look into the globe and see things that are hidden from normal sight. Not everyone could use the globe in this way, only someone gifted from birth, as I am. I can see things that *might* happen, and use a kind of magic to make sure they either do or don't happen.'

He paused and took a sip of his wine. I realised he was avoiding looking me in the eye.

'My mother would be horrified if she knew I was telling you this. She knows of my special gifts but we never discuss it. She is a good Christian, who believes that her faith in Christ is enough.'

'Then why are you telling me?' I was angry. I

had to be faithful to my mistress and also to Arthur. Now I was being asked to keep secrets from them!

'Simply this: I may be able to find the golden torc, but I need your help. Oh yes, ' he added, seeing the astonished look on my face, 'I am sure it exists, and is somewhere nearby. That much I have discovered by my arts.'

'Then why didn't you already go and find it yourself? You could have saved us a lot of trouble!'

Magnus gave a dry chuckle. 'Vibiana, I am not all-powerful! I do not know exactly where it is, and I cannot be seen crawling around looking for it. I need someone to be my ears and eyes and hands, to go places where I cannot.'

'You have Gruffin.'

'I cannot count on his intelligence, or his secrecy. He might overlook the thing I need, or else blurt it out to the wrong person. I can trust you.'

I folded my arms and glared at him.

'You do want Arthur to be king?'

I nodded.

'And if we can find the torc, no matter how we find it, the kingdom is won fairly?'

Slowly, I nodded again.

'All right then, I will help you. Tell me what I have to do.' I knew it was right, to do anything to help Arthur. Then why were my insides suddenly churning, as if I'd eaten rotten fish? I thought of something else. 'But it's all for nothing! Arthur will lose tomorrow to Taran!'

Magnus gave a secretive smile. 'Perhaps, perhaps not. Wait and see.'

'And the globe? You said you see things in it, but also that you can make things happen, like someone throwing that stone at Taran.'

The teacher shrugged slightly and I knew I would get no more from him that night. I still wanted to know more, but now my curiosity was mixed with fear. If I couldn't talk to Arthur or Zea about it, who could I turn to?

One More Week

*At least we have one more week.
I have decided to pray every night,
because I do not know what else to do.
That, and keep my eyes wide open.*

Everything was different. Yes, the place was the
same, but nothing else. It was damp and foggy, the
trees bordering the training field dripping drearily
with too much water. A small crowd had gathered
but no servants, only the warriors and those of us
who were friends of Arthur. I didn't see Morcanta
and that made me nervous. What was she up to? I
was sure she would be here.

Caradoc beat his palms on Arthur's back to warm
him up. Arthur was wrapped in a cloak of red wool
which stood out in the gloom like the plumage of a
bright bird. I tried to take this colour as a good
omen. Taran was already stripped, strutting around
preening and showing off his muscles. Neither
Arthur nor Taran had their skin oiled this time. There
must have been some agreement about that.

Rhys and Magnus stood in the centre of the circle,
talking in low voices. They seemed to be arguing
something. I tried not to look at Magnus because
whenever I did, I had that sick feeling again. I know he
was just asking me to look for the torc in places that he
told me to. But I also knew that some dark arts were
behind it. If I had asked Zea, she would have said to
run from it. I wondered what Brendan would say.

I didn't plan to tell Arthur either. He wouldn't
agree to Magnus using ancient magic even for such a

good cause, I was sure of that. If he weren't so honest and true, things would be simpler – but of course I was very glad he was. I sucked in a deep breath and tried to stay calm.

'It is time!' Rhys said. The crowd congealed into two distinct groups, each backing the man they supported. Arthur removed his cloak and shifted lightly from one foot to the other. Taran stopped flexing his muscles and stood still, looking even more menacing in the dim light than he had before in the bright sun at the first combat.

Magnus stepped forward and gave his little speech, then the two combatants faced off.

This time instead of murmured encouragement from the crowd there was near silence, only an intake of breath when the two lunged forward. They grappled and for some moments it was like a scene frozen in ice: two bodies wrapped around each other, neither giving way. The sword Caliburn was laid out on the flat boulder, waiting silently for the victor.

Then with a flick of one foot Taran sent Arthur flying on his back and raised his arms in triumph. At that, the silence broke and his men cheered.

'Arthur! Arthur! Get up, you can do it!' our side shouted.

Arthur rolled on his front and hopped lightly to his feet. He hardly seemed winded. I breathed again.

The two danced around each other, waiting for the right moment. They were poorly matched. It was hardly a fair fight, Taran easily doubled Arthur in weight, although Arthur had a slight advantage with speed and agility. And Arthur had all the experience of a few weeks, compared to years for

Taran! I thought of shouting out my protest but knew that would offend Arthur. I was his friend; I ought to believe he could win.

Now! They met, Arthur tripped Taran this time! Maybe he was learning as he fought, but it wouldn't be enough. Taran was down on his face, Arthur had one of his opponent's muscular arms pinned behind him. We were all yelling madly but almost before we got a sound out, Taran used his other arm to flip himself over and flick Arthur off his back like he was a slightly irritating bug. Arthur flew several feet to one side and skidded to a stop on his bottom.

Taran's people jeered and laughed and started making rude jokes. The rest of us went completely silent.

Arthur blushed bright red as he got to his feet and dusted himself off. For the third time, the two faced off, circling each other.

'Arthur, you can win!' I shouted into the silence.

Before Taran realised what was happening, Arthur slipped behind him and jumped on his back, his legs squeezing Taran's waist. I laughed at the sight of Arthur's slender pale legs wrapping like vines around Taran's tanned body. But then I held my breath as Taran began to tug at Arthur's legs.

'Tighter, Arthur, tighter!' I shouted.

Arthur boxed Taran's ears. Without warning, Taran flipped his hands up to grab Arthur's head, yanking sharply so that Arthur's forehead rammed into the back of Taran's skull.

Both sides yelled in fear or hope. There was a brief pause, then Arthur slid down Taran's back and lay senseless in the dirt. I ran forward, ignoring stern calls ordering me back. I knelt by my friend but didn't touch him. I put my face next to his, waited until I was sure I felt his breath on my cheek, then stood up.

'He lives.'

I returned to my place, ignoring cat-calls from Taran's men. Again Taran circled the ring, arms raised in triumph, as his men called out 'Victory to Taran! He has won fairly; give him the sword!'

The warrior Rhys looked to Magnus, who nodded. I tried to read the wise man's face. I wasn't sure, but it looked like he was still waiting for something to happen.

Rhys moved to the stone where the ancient sword rested. Arthur lay in the dirt, not moving. Would it end like this? I couldn't accept that.

'Wait!' I shouted.

Rhys tried to ignore me. He picked up the sword and carried it flat in both hands into the centre. Taran waited confidently next to Magnus to receive his prize.

'Speak, Vibiana,' Magnus said, holding up one hand to Rhys.

I stepped forward. 'The fight was fair,' I began, trying keep my voice from shaking, 'but is this the right way to grant victory?' I pointed to Arthur laid out flat on the damp earth. 'When Arthur awakes, he will not question Taran's win. But let all be done decently, in front of everyone. Let Arthur himself give Caliburn to Taran. Otherwise, won't people whisper and say it was done behind Arthur's back?'

There was silence. Magnus' face creased in a slow smile. I dared to glance around. Many were nodding, and not just those on our side. Taran glared at Magnus and Rhys.

These two put their heads together for a quick discussion.

'Taran is victor,' Magnus announced finally. 'The kingdom is his. At a feast this day next week, Arthur will present the winner with Caliburn.'

There was a bit of half-hearted clapping from Taran's men. At least their favourite won, even if official victory was delayed. Cai and I ran to Arthur, who was already attended by Caradoc. Two warriors brought a litter.

'Should I fetch the doctor?'

Caradoc shook his head. 'His colour is good. I'll watch by his bed until he wakes.'

'I'll be with Zea, but please send for me if you need to.'

Caradoc nodded grimly and turned to direct the men to lift Arthur carefully onto the litter. He followed them with bowed head as they carried the litter back to the villa, and I thought he looked older all of a sudden. This meant the end of all his hopes, all the work he had put into training Arthur.

Only I wasn't so sure about that. True, Taran had won fairly, but this didn't feel like the end to me. We had a week; anything could happen!

But where was Morcanta? I decided to watch her more closely. I was sure she hadn't given up her craving to rule the kingdom of Caerleon.

Message in Song

Magnus said to keep my eyes open.
It was not my eyes I needed to
have open, but my ears!

'Lady said Bem come today.'

'What lady is that?' asked Arthur.

'She with red hair. I sit by her fire, sing to her.'
Bem sat up from his cushion and clicked his tongue
for Stinker.

All around us servants hurried back and forth in
the long dining room with ladders and cloths,
dusting up to the very rafters in preparation for
tomorrow's feast. A huge bronze brazier filled with
glowing charcoal was set on a low platform in the
middle of the room. We had drawn up cushions
near the brazier. Stinker lay with all four legs
stretched out stiffly, as close as possible to the
warmth.

'Don't go, Bem! Stay here and sing for us,' I
urged. 'Do you have a new song?'

Arthur lay stretched out on two cushions, gazing
blankly into the fire. He didn't even seem to hear
what we said.

'Let them go – it's starting to smell in here!' Cai
was concentrating on whittling an animal out of a
chunk of wood. At the moment it looked like no
animal I'd ever seen.

He was wrong, though. For once the smell had
nothing to do with Stinker. The long room reeked

of charcoal smoke, scented oil used to rub the wooden beams and freshly washed tiles.

Arthur had awoken in the evening after the conflict. I wasn't there so I don't know how he took the news that he would lose Caliburn and the kingship, but since then he'd been more quiet, sometimes sighing at nothing.

'Sing it for us first,' I repeated.

Bem smiled and nodded. He cocked his head to the right so that his ear almost touched his shoulder, and began to sing in his clear, pure voice:

> *In the ancient wood he stood*
> *saw the silver stream in a dream*
> *found the pond with oaks ringed round*
> *took precious gold from the ground.*

> *Two men fought in a field*
> *and the strong man won;*
> *but the one with the ring of gold*
> *is the king's own son.*

This he repeated several times in different forms, with tunes rising and falling. Bem was gifted in music, we'd always known that. Just now I was thinking about the words.

'Very nice,' Arthur said, yawning. Cai nodded, then swore as he sliced his finger with the knife.

'It's the same song we heard before, with some words added,' I said.

Bem smiled happily and began all over again.

'Don't sing it for us. Go on and find the Lady, sing it for her. She'll be very pleased!'

103

Cai stopped whittling and raised his eyebrows as I said this. Arthur was tracing the pattern of mosaic on the floor with his finger and didn't seem to hear.

Immediately Bem struggled to his feet and shuffled off. Stinker raised his head and sighed, then dropped it down again. It was too cosy by the fire.

I waited a few moments then got to my feet. 'I must see to Zea.' I left quickly, following Bem. He was speaking with a servant girl in the doorway of Morcanta's quarters, then changed direction and headed for the kitchen. I followed.

That was my charge from Magnus: to keep an eye on Arthur, and also to try and find out what Morcanta was up to. He had sent another servant girl to sit every day with Zea, who was well enough to be in her chair some of the day, and just wanted a bit of company.

'Arthur is the centre,' Magnus had said. 'He must be king. It is his destiny. Morcanta will try to stop it; Taran believes he already has. Arthur has given up. I need you to be very watchful. Something will happen, and you must bring me word when it does.'

All week long I had lurked as near Morcanta as I dared, without success. The first day, I came upon Morcanta whispering with one of her women, the one with the pock-marked face. She was leaving the king's quarters. The woman was reaching inside the pocket of her robe when she saw me and quickly withdrew her hand.

'Vibiana,' Morcanta said coldly, 'Zea has sent for you. Go quickly, she is not well.'

'She was well this morning.'

But what if something had happened? I raced

back to Zea, but she was nodding in her chair while the servant girl brushed her hair. When I ran back to accuse Morcanta of lying, she and the other woman had disappeared.

What was her woman doing in the king's quarters? Something important, that needed a lie to get rid of me. Arthur had a chamber there, which he shared with Cai. I would mention this to him, ask him if he noticed anything missing.

Now as I followed Bem, I was more careful. There were some empty baskets lying near the open door of the kitchen and I picked one up.

Even from outside I could hear Morcanta chiding Fulvia. 'The sauce always runs out before the meal is half done!'

I hooked the basket over my arm and stepped inside. Morcanta towered over the cook, but she didn't seem bothered. Fulvia was a sturdy woman, probably well used to dealing with Morcanta.

'We make the sauce as always, in the largest pot. They must be bathing in it, to make it go so fast.'

Morcanta's green eyes flashed a warning. 'See to it that you make *two* pots tomorrow. Three, if needed! I don't want to have to send for you in the middle of the feast, to find out why we have no more sauce!'

Fulvia barely nodded and turned away. Morcanta opened her mouth to protest when Bem touched her sleeve.

'Lady, Bem will sing song for you!'

She transformed on the spot from a witch to something like a tame kitten.

'Bem,' she said in a silvery voice, 'wait for me. I am eager to hear it!'

She turned back to continue her tirade, but Fulvia had wisely moved out of reach and was tasting something from a pot simmering on the vast brick stove. I busied myself with selecting some dried herbs hanging from the rafters, hoping Morcanta wouldn't notice me.

Behind me, Bem began to sing:

> *Two men fought in a field*
> *and the strong man won;*
> *but the one with the ring of gold*
> *is the king's own son.*

I needn't have worried. As soon as she heard that, Morcanta took Bem by the arm and nearly dragged him out the door.

'Come! You will sing for me, and I will give you honeyed figs.'

I waited for a moment, then peered out. Morcanta was almost running towards her quarters with Bem limping awkwardly to keep up. I couldn't simply follow them into her chamber. I headed back to the dining room, trying to think of a plan. Maybe Cai could help me. Arthur wasn't much good for thinking at the moment, but he might be able to get into Morcanta's room without making her suspicious.

'What's the basket for?' Cai wondered. He held up his carved animal for me to see.

'A pig?'

'A horse, stupid!'

'Oh.' I flopped down in one of the chairs by the

fire and tossed the basket aside. Arthur seemed to be asleep.

'Is something wrong?' Cai asked.

'We need a way to get into Morcanta's room.'

'Why?'

'She's up to something. Don't you think it's strange she doesn't seem worried that she's lost the kingdom? Right now she's got Bem with her, listening to his song. There's a meaning to it, or at least she thinks so. She's trying to use Bem.'

'Meaning to the song? Use Bem? What are you babbling about?' Cai gave a disgusted flick of the knife and his 'horse' was headless.

'Listen.' I leaned forward. 'We don't have much time. Tomorrow night, Arthur hands the kingdom over to Taran.' It was blunt, but I hoped to shock Arthur out of his stupor. He sat up and scowled at me. That was a start, at least! Cai frowned, his dark eyebrows nearly meeting.

'Think about what Bem was singing: gold found in a wood, something about a pond, then a fight between two men, one is the king's son.'

'One has the ring of gold! I remember that bit.'

'Ring of gold,' I repeated. 'Does that suggest anything to you?'

'The torc,' Arthur whispered.

'He speaks!' I exclaimed. Arthur managed a grin. 'Can you think of an excuse to go and see Morcanta now?'

Arthur paused. It struck me how pale and pinched his face looked. 'I can speak with her about what she and I will do, after Taran is made king. I should have done that in any case.'

'Let's go!' Cai said, leaping to his feet.

'No! It's better if Arthur goes alone, quietly.' I added, 'Enter slowly, hear what Morcanta is saying to Bem if you can.'

While we waited for Arthur to return, Cai picked up his whittling again, obviously intent on turning it into a mouse. I stroked Stinker's wiry fur with my foot and stared into the fire.

Then Arthur was back, too quickly it seemed to me.

'What happened?'

He sat down beside me. 'Bem wasn't there.'

'Where was he?'

'Off on an errand for her, she said. She was very mysterious about it.'

'Did you talk to her at all?' Cai asked.

'That was the strange thing.' Arthur leaned forward, the firelight giving warmth to his cheeks. 'She didn't want to talk about what would happen after Taran became king.'

'Why not?' I demanded.

'She just said, "You talk of *our* defeat – perhaps we should talk of what happens to you, after *my* victory!'

Missing

Should I place the blame on a dog?
No, it is our fault for not thinking ahead,
watching more carefully.

Queen Aurelia never appeared in public any more, but Arthur said she had decided to attend the feast that night.

'It's only right she should be there when the kingdom passes out of our family. And Caliburn.'

He swallowed hard and I didn't know what to say. I wanted to clap him on the shoulder and tell him to cheer up, say something about how it wouldn't be so bad, everything would work out for the best. But I didn't believe it, and neither would he. How could things be worse than they were at this moment?

We sat on the edge of the courtyard veranda, watching servants scurrying to and fro. Morcanta had decided to invite important people from the town, as well as everyone from the High Hill. It seemed she was eager to have the whole of Caerleon present when Taran was made king, which didn't sound like her at all.

I wondered if Llian would come down, or if she would be left all alone there, praying while the rest of us celebrated. I wouldn't feel much like celebrating, that was certain.

Just then Morcanta breezed past, her green gown flowing out behind her. She didn't notice us until Arthur spoke.

'Morcanta.'

She stopped, obviously unwilling to spare him even a moment. Arthur stood, and I noticed he was taller than she was.

'My mother has decided to attend the festivities.'

'She never leaves your father's side!' The tip of her nose turned pink.

'No, but tonight she will.' Arthur spoke fiercely, punching out the words. 'It is proper for the queen to attend when she is being deprived of her heritage!'

'Through no fault of *mine.*'

Arthur flinched but stood his ground. 'Nor did I say that. The blame is fully mine. Please see to it that the queen's place at the head table is ready for her?'

She nodded and moved quickly on, her red hair shining in the autumn sun.

'Why was she upset about your mother coming to the feast?'

'Do you think she was?'

'Oh yes. It wasn't just you giving her an order, or that she didn't want to be bothered preparing your mother's place. Did you notice how quickly she turned away?'

He shook his head, as puzzled as I was. 'Come,' he said.

I followed him into the dining room where long tables were arranged in an open square around the room. People would sit at benches except for those at the top, where the very important guests would sit in carved chairs and eat out of silver dishes.

Arthur signed to Justus, who joined us.

'Bring the queen's chair.'

The overseer looked startled but he nodded and ordered a servant to fetch the chair. It was kept in the storehouse, so that no one else would sit in it by mistake if the queen was not there. At the centre of the head table was the king's chair.

'Why–' I started to ask a question but caught myself. I felt my face glowing red. Arthur lifted his chin and pretended not to hear. Of course! The king's chair was there for Taran. It would remain empty I guessed, until Taran was officially made king. Taran, made king! It didn't bear thinking about. He was a rough bear of a man, clever and a good warrior, but never a king! Queen Aurelia would have to sit next to him, too. I wished she'd change her mind about coming; it wouldn't be easy for her to look at her husband's place and see Taran instead.

Until recently, I had ignored Zea's instruction to pray about Arthur finding the torc and becoming king, but surely lots of other people were praying! How could the Lord God have overlooked this? Even Magnus, who did not pray, said that being king was Arthur's destiny. If it was his destiny but it didn't happen, where did that leave him? Arthur would be – what? One of Taran's warriors? His advisor, perhaps, when he was older. Someone who could read and write and give counsel. But he wouldn't be king. Not the good and powerful ruler he was meant to be.

A sound made me turn. Before I realised what it was, I thought for an instant of clear water running over stones in a brook.

'Brendan, greetings!' I called in Latin.

Brendan grinned and joined us, strumming his colourful harp.

'Vibiana, I have not seen you. I thought you would come to the Abbey sometimes.'

'I almost came one day, but something happened. This is Arthur.' As the two greeted each other, I hoped Brendan wouldn't ask who Arthur was. What would I say, he's the prince but not for long? Fortunately either Brendan already knew or he didn't think it was important.

'Will you play for the feast tonight?'

Brendan nodded, his grey eyes gleaming. 'Listen! Let me practice for you.'

We seated ourselves on one of the benches, and Brendan began to play and sing a haunting song in his own language. By the time he finished, I had tears in my eyes and Arthur was white as a newborn lamb.

'What does it mean?' Arthur asked.

Brendan smiled and ran a hand through his tangled brown curls. 'I made it myself. The words in my language are better, but it is something like this:

Come Lord Christ,
you who ride on the clouds,
you who soar with the wild geese
to heaven and live in Heaven,
and made the birds and the clouds:
you who walked on earth as a man,
and made the earth and fire:
come give us your Spirit,
come show us your love,
come live in us, so we may live in you.

'Do you like it?' he asked anxiously, as both of us were quiet.

'Very much.' It was more than that, but I didn't know how to say it. I had the oddest sensation inside, like being given an unexpected present and at the same time, having an itchy feeling, as if I was about to catch a fever.

'The Lord helps me,' said Brendan. 'He has given me the gift of music, and sometimes he brings melodies and words to my minds. I cannot help it!'

He laughed and strummed the harp, making a sound like birds calling on the wind.

I glanced at Arthur. His eyes were flecked with yellow and he gazed at nothing. I wanted to talk with him, but not in Latin.

'Will you pardon us if we talk for a time in our language?'

Brendan nodded and moved away to another bench where he sat playing softly.

We listened for a while, then Arthur spoke.

'Remember, Vibiana, when you asked me if I truly believed in the teachings of Christ.'

'I remember.'

'And I laughed at you for thinking there could be more to belief than what we know: chapel morning and evening, saying our prayers, helping the poor. These are good things, what I was always taught, and I thought they were enough.

'But this boy –'

'Brendan.'

'Yes, this Brendan and for all I know, all who live in the Abbey or the monks who crossed the sea to come here, perhaps they've found something more. The Lord Christ seems so real to them, almost like a friend they know.'

'You're right! Maybe that's why – well, why some people live in a place of prayer and never come out.'

'It seems to me, if we are to be good Christians, we should learn more about this way of faith. If I am to lead the people, I must be–'

At the look on my face, he stopped.

'Oh. Right. I keep forgetting.'

'Something will happen!' I exclaimed. 'It has to! You will be king someday, maybe Taran will take Caerleon now, but when you are older there will be another combat between the two of you, or he will die in battle, there's a thought! He has no children, then you will be king!'

Arthur laughed in spite of himself. Over the noise of preparation for the feast came a muffled honking sound which got louder and louder until it was right overhead.

Arthur and I ran outside and Brendan joined us.

'The wild geese,' Brendan murmured as we watched the great birds sailing over us, winging their way south.

'Do you believe they are an omen?'

Brendan grinned at me. I noticed that his eyes were the same grey-brown colour of the flying geese. 'No, any more than I believe if you cut one open, you can read your future in its guts. The wild geese remind us of God's spirit, high and free, not tamed by us but winging the whole earth.

'God's Spirit sent us here,' he added.

'I thought Abbot Feoras already knew the Abbess, came to visit her,' I said.

'No. We prayed to be led, and this is where the winds and tides brought us.'

'I would learn more of this,' Arthur said.

'Feoras would teach you, if you ask him.'

'But perhaps I will have no use for the knowledge.' The corners of Arthur's mouth drooped. I wanted to cheer him up, but what was there to say?

'Of course you will need it!' Brendan said. 'Every person who belongs to Christ should seek to learn and grow in him. The Lord is like a friend to me. I can talk to him whenever I want, and I try to listen to his voice. Sometimes I feel him nudging me to do a certain thing or sometimes *not* to do something.'

Arthur and I were silent. I think we were both envious. What must it be like, to have a friend that close?

Cai burst onto us, breaking our stillness. He was dragging Stinker with a bit of rope tied around his neck. The dog whined pitifully, trying to pull in the opposite direction.

'Bem is missing!' he exclaimed. 'I've asked everywhere, no one's seen him since he left yesterday heading for Caerleon town on an errand for Morcanta.

'And the gatekeeper says Stinker has been running in and out of the villa compound all day. Something must have happened to him!'

A Challenge I Can't Accept

I should go on praying, but something
stops me. I keep thinking of the
person who disappointed me.

'We've got to find him!' I exclaimed.

'If he's left Stinker behind–' Cai began.

'Stinker can lead us to him,' Arthur said. 'Maybe he's lying injured somewhere.'

I hoped that was the worst we would find. Bem and Stinker were never apart for long. I was sure Morcanta had something to do with this.

Cai slipped the noose off Stinker's head. He whined sharply and began to whirl in circles in the dirt, moaning and squealing like a wounded boar.

'Go, Stinker!' Arthur urged. 'Find Bem!'

The dog gave an excited bark and bounded away.

Before Arthur or Cai could collect their wits, I started running. Stinker pelted across the courtyard, knocking flat a servant girl carrying a basket of washing. She lay in the dust and wailed as the ground was littered with wet clothes, but I didn't stop to help. With Arthur and Cai pounding along behind, I kept my eyes on the bouncing brown lump that was Stinker. The gatekeeper opened his mouth as I dashed by him, but I just kept on running. Stinker darted across the newly repaired bridge to Caerleon town, dodging carts and horses. I caught up with him downstream on the opposite bank of the river. He was whining anxiously and pacing back and forth.

'Good boy!' I patted his head. 'Where's Bem? Show us where he is!'

Arthur skidded to a halt next to me. 'Can't he find him?'

'He came straight here, but now he's confused.'

The River Usk gurgled along, still swollen from the floods. 'Could Bem paddle a boat?'

'I don't think so. I've never seen him even go near the water, except to cross the bridge.'

Cai joined us, panting as hard as Stinker. Brendan wasn't far behind, minus his harp and with the skirt of his robe tucked up into his belt.

'I think someone took Bem away in a boat,' Arthur said. 'That's why Stinker didn't find him. I bet he's been down here looking, only we never noticed. Haven't you, boy?' He rubbed Stinker's ears but the dog just kept staring out at the water.

'If he went in a boat, we'll never find him!' I said.

All of a sudden I pictured Bem being led away by some evil person, still smiling, not understanding that anyone would want to harm him. 'He might be dead!'

'What is happening?' Brendan asked. Arthur explained in Latin.

'I will ask the brothers to pray for Bem. God will help us find him.'

'Yes,' said Arthur. 'We must pray. What else is there to do?'

After a moment I nodded. 'We will come with you to the Abbey. I know someone else there who will pray.'

Cai slipped the rope over Stinker's head again and Brendan unhitched his brown robe from his belt.

'Did Morcanta tell you what Bem's errand was?' I asked Arthur, as the four of us walked back past the villa and up the hill to the Abbey enclosure. Stinker seemed calmer now and trotted along beside Cai.

He shook his head. 'I should have asked her, but I had other things on my mind.'

'Why would she send him?' asked Cai. 'She has plenty of servants.'

'Maybe they were all busy preparing for the feast,' I said.

'Or maybe,' Arthur said, 'she simply wanted to get him out of the way for some reason. I'm sure she wouldn't harm him.'

'I'm not!' I said. 'I know she's your step-sister, but I don't trust her. She'd do anything to be able to rule Caerleon! I think she's up to something. Why hasn't she protested more at the idea of Taran becoming king? I expected her to gather her supporters together and attack the villa! But no, she's simply gone on as before, being the mistress of the villa while your mother takes care of your father.'

Arthur frowned as he considered what I said. 'You're right. It should have occurred to me. Why hasn't Morcanta done something? She's been as meek as a weaned calf!'

'She doesn't have enough supporters to win a battle,' Cai said. 'Most of them are women, anyway.

Sorry,' he added, glancing at me. 'None of them are as well trained as you, Vibiana!'

'Never mind. The point is, what is she about to do? Even Magnus thinks she's up to something.'

'You didn't tell me that!' Arthur said.

'Didn't want to worry you. You know now! What can we do, besides watch her carefully?'

I glanced at Brendan, who followed us silently. He smiled at me. Then I realised he didn't understand what we were saying, because we hadn't bothered to speak Latin. I dropped back to walk beside him, explaining as best I could.

'So Arthur would be king if he found the torc, even though Taran has won the combat.'

'Yes, I think so. Taran and the Council of Elders agreed originally to Morcanta's challenge to find the torc. The idea of a combat came later. It was something dreamed up by Taran as a quick way to gain power.'

'Then we must pray that the torc is found, as well as Bem!'

I didn't understand how the God who made this world and the people in it, could be bothered to go out looking for one lost person or object.

'What if they are not?'

Brendan grinned at that. 'Can you accept a challenge, Vibiana?'

'Of course! What is it?'

'I challenge you to pray with someone. Maybe this person you said would pray also, at the Abbey. One of the nuns? Tell her of the need, pray with her. The Lord Christ has promised to be present in a special way with even two people who meet to pray.'

'Does that mean he will definitely lead us to Bem and the torc?'

Brendan shook his head. 'No. We do not know or see everything that he does. He may have reasons why we do not find them.

'But prayer is like a strong cord that ties us to him and to each other. Without it, we drift away. We of the community pray together for three hours each evening, before bed.'

'Three hours!' No wonder I didn't see much of Llian.

He smiled. 'It does not seem so long. Sometimes we sing as well. For me, I could put all my prayers into song, but I do not, for the sake of the others.'

'Why not? I would never get tired of listening to you.'

As we neared the Abbey enclosure Brendan began to tell me what he had heard of the Druid's Wood beyond it.

'Those of the Abbey have warned us not to go there. The Druids – you know of them surely, the ancient priests of our peoples – they sacrificed animals or children to their gods, or threw their treasures into the sacred pond to keep the gods happy. Of course that was long ago, but still it is good to avoid these places – they hold echoes of their evil past.'

His voice trickled on and on like a flowing stream. These were things I'd already heard and I didn't pay much attention; my mind wandered to Llian, and I saw that my picture of her life in the Abbey was not accurate. It was not so much being alone, but being with a group of people, all working together, praying together. I began to think it was a good thing for her, even if it meant I didn't have a mother.

That reminded me that she chose for some reason to stay on the High Hill, never once coming down to see me. I was her daughter! Did I mean so little to her?

By the time we reached the wattle fence I had made myself angry with Llian all over again, and was in no mood to ask her anything.

The Spider Spins Her Web

I knew it all along! Days ago in this record,
I wrote of the spider spinning her web.
I have no joy in being right.

A few hens clucked and scampered out of our way as
Arthur pushed open the gate. When we entered the
enclosure they settled down and continued their
pecking in the grass beside the neatly tended stone
pathway. No one was about, so we went to the small
stone chapel. The door was open and we could see it
was empty except for several robed men lying face
down on the stone floor before the altar. By their
long hair I recognised them as monks from Hibernia.

'Where is everyone?' Cai asked.

'In the refectory, I think,' Brendan said. 'It is
warm there, and a good place for all to meet.'

It was the round hut between the two long ones.
Arthur paused in the doorway, then we heard a
woman bid him enter.

He stepped inside, and we followed. With its
small windows the refectory would have been dark
except for the many rush lamps on the tables, which
were set up in the shape of a square. The walls were
bare whitewashed wattle and daub, with only a
single wooden cross hanging on the wall opposite
the door. The place had a clean smell, as if dirt was
not allowed to enter there.

The monk Feoras sat next to Abbess Brangwen
at the head table beneath the cross. The men from
Hibernia ranged around to the left of Feoras, and

those of the Abbey community, men and women, sat to the right of the Abbess. I let my glance slide across them and knew that Llian was there, but I didn't look at her directly.

Plain wooden plates and bowls on the table held the remains of a simple meal.

'We are sorry to interrupt,' Arthur said.

'You would not come here without good reason,' said the Abbess, motioning us to a bench next to the monks from Hibernia. She frowned slightly at the sight of Stinker, and Cai quickly dragged him outside to tie him up before joining us.

As soon as we had settled ourselves, Abbess Brangwen asked Arthur to speak.

'We have come with a special petition. A man is missing, and we would ask for prayer that he might be found.'

Arthur hesitated. I thought he might as well go on and tell the whole story.

'We will pray for him,' said the Abbess, looking around at the others. All nodded and murmured their agreement.

'It is Bem,' Arthur went on, and there were several exclamations at this. Bem was probably well known here, as he would have no shyness about wandering in.

After Arthur explained as much as we knew, the Abbess looked at him with a kind yet piercing gaze. Today she wore a simple brown belted robe and seemed more like a grandmother. Feoras sitting beside her did not speak, but his face showed he was listening intently.

'My son, I believe there is more,' Abbess Brangwen said.

Slowly, Arthur stood and took a deep breath. But what he said next was not at all what I expected.

'I have seen that you of the community and you men from Hibernia, have a faith that we here in Caerleon have not known. I believe our people need to learn the way of Christ more fully. We lack something that you can give us, if you will.'

He waited during the moment of quiet that followed. Abbess Brangwen smiled gently. A few of the monks from Hibernia nodded, but most looked to their leader, to see if he would respond. Feoras raised his eyebrows at the Abbess, who inclined her head. Feoras stood up. He was easily the tallest person in the room. I felt an unusual stillness in this man, but also great power.

'I am sure the Lord Christ whom I serve is pleased with your request, Prince Arthur of Caerleon. Even now, on the day when your kingdom will pass to the hands of another, you think of your people. God will bless you for this.

'We men of Hibernia have been sent here for a reason,' Feoras went on. 'We have waited and prayed these many days, to know what is to be our task in this place. I believe now, in your request, we have the answer.'

He sat down, and turned to his followers. He seemed to be searching the face of each one for agreement. Feoras nodded, apparently satisfied with what he saw.

Abbess Brangwen stood.

'Prince Arthur, I too believe the Lord Christ is

pleased with your petition. We will think and pray together how this will be accomplished. Glyneth, bring refreshment for all!'

Over beakers of ale, we spent an hour in the room with everyone adding their own thoughts, presided over by the Abbess. No one's words were treated as stupid, but all were made to feel what they said was important. One idea was that there could be a kind of school, where the monks could teach the people of Caerleon.

By the end Arthur had invited them all to the feast. Abbess Brangwen declined on behalf of the community, saying it wouldn't be appropriate for them to begin in haste doing something so opposite to their normal way of life. They would remain on the hill, praying for Bem.

'However,' she added, 'it is good that the men of Hibernia join the feast. We have too long been completely separate. One cannot change old ways too quickly, but you will open the door for us. Who knows what will come of it? I believe this was a most blessed encounter, Prince Arthur of Caerleon!'

Arthur thanked her but I saw pain in his eyes. The title of 'prince' was one he would wear for only a few hours more.

As we left the hut, I noticed the Abbess motion Llian to her side. I had not spoken to my mother or even acknowledged her. I was still angry with her for cutting herself off from me so thoroughly. I put from my mind Brendan's challenge to pray with one of the nuns. Something inside was telling me I should be more sensible about it, but I didn't want to be!

*

We hadn't seen such a feast at the villa since I was a little girl, when King Uther was well and strong and ruling all Caerleon. How things could change! The peace and safety of that time was only a distant memory. Then, my father was alive and the three of us lived happily. Everyone thought Arthur would become king after his father, and anyway that was all far in the future. We expected to continue many years in the security of that life.

Now, even in the midst of drinking and eating and loud laughter from the many guests, there was a whisper of fear and suspicion. I don't mean anything spoken out loud, but something underneath. Was it simply my imagination? I looked to the head table, trying to read the expressions beneath festive faces.

Queen Aurelia's face was the colour of parchment. Was that only because she hadn't seen the sun in so long through sitting all day by her dying husband? Her robe was the colour of rich cream, decorated in fine gold embroidery, with a deep blue shawl pinned at the shoulder by an intricate brooch. Her clothes only served to highlight her pallor and the grey tinge to her hair. She wore no jewellery except the brooch; that gave her a bare look, as if she had already given up her right to be queen.

Arthur sat next to his mother, proud and straight. I could guess the turmoil in his heart, not betrayed by his blank face.

Next to the queen, the king's chair made an empty space in the centre of the table. Taran seated to the right of it sounded half-drunk as he laughed and clanged his silver beaker on the table. I noticed he'd refused the imported wine offered to those at the head table, drinking deeply of the ale and hailing the servants for more. I reckoned he was one person here who was truly enjoying himself! Magnus was next to him, looking official and Roman in a white woollen robe trimmed with blue. I couldn't read his face.

Morcanta puzzled me. Seated to Arthur's left, she wore a dress of forest green edged with gold, and a purple shawl wrapped around her neck instead of pinned to her shoulder. It looked very odd. Her expression worried me. I thought she was excited about something and was trying not to let it show.

As servants brought platters of roast dormice, snails and peacocks' eggs for starters, they had to weave their way around the centrepiece of the room, a small table where Caliburn rested on a red cushion. Every time Taran raised his cup, he saluted the sword which waited for him. Arthur stared straight ahead or at his plate, trying not to see this.

I sat at one of the tables along the rear wall, with Cai and Brendan on either side. We didn't talk much. Even Brendan was quiet, except when he played and sang. There was a sadness in his songs that didn't suit the mood of a feast, yet somehow it was right. I looked up during one song and saw tears running unchecked down the queen's face.

More courses followed: roast boar, swan, hare and frogs; honey cakes and fruits for dessert.

At last, Magnus stood and lifted his hand for silence. Even after the whole room was quiet,

Magnus paused. Once again I had the feeling he was waiting for something to happen.

'People of Caerleon,' he said, 'the moment has come to appoint our ruler! We are grateful for the long and faithful rule of Uther and his queen.'

At this Magnus gave a deep bow to Queen Aurelia and the whole company clapped and cheered. The queen smiled weakly and nodded her thanks.

'Now, through fair combat, the kingship passes to another. Bring Caliburn!'

Rhys stepped forward and lifted the long sword from its place. He carried it with arms stretched out to the head table, facing Taran who stood as Rhys approached.

Magnus opened his mouth to declare Taran ruler, when suddenly Morcanta stood. All eyes snapped in her direction, and Taran realised something was wrong. He whirled around. When he saw who it was his face turned red as wine.

'Wait!' Morcanta's voice pierced the silence like a blow from Caliburn itself.

'The combat between Taran and my brother was fair. But the ruler of Caerleon, according to the will of the Council, is the one who finds the lost torc of our ancestors. That person is the one chosen by the gods!'

With a flourish, she pulled the purple shawl from her neck. Around it a circle of twisted gold, thick as a snake, shone like the sun. Morcanta had found the torc.

In Over My Head

*I hear Zea snoring behind the curtain.
I cannot write down everything. There are
some things I could never, ever risk telling.*

A loud gasp, then dead silence.

'This must be proven,' Magnus said quickly.

The room burst into a blare of noise, some shouting for Taran, Morcanta's friends clapping and cheering. Over it all, Taran bellowed furiously.

'No! I am by rights – it is my right –'

He swung his arms, knocking over the long table. Plates and platters smashed to the floor and most of us jumped up ready to fight or at least wanting to see everything, whatever would happen. Stinker had been asleep under my feet; he leaped up and added his barking to the noise.

With a roar of anger, Taran swept past Arthur and clamped his hands around Morcanta's white neck, pressing the torc into her flesh. Her scream was choked off in a horrible gagging sound. Arthur and several warlords leaped on Taran and pried his fingers loose. Morcanta staggered back, clutching at her throat.

'Take him away!' She tried to shout the order but it sounded like a frog call.

The warlords led Taran from the room. No one jeered at this; I think they were all afraid of him, even if some might have been glad to see him defeated.

But Morcanta as ruler! Who could want that? Only the handful of fierce-looking women who clustered around her, straightening her garments and offering her wine. One of the women gently removed the torc. Morcanta's throat bore harsh red marks from the metal.

Meanwhile, servants righted the table and cleared away dented silver dishes and the remains of food. Arthur guided his mother out of the room; she looked dazed and shaky. The feast was over.

Magnus announced, 'The Council will meet tomorrow to discuss this.' There were murmurs of agreement.

'Will Morcanta take the kingdom?' Cai asked. He was breathless from translating everything quickly for Brendan.

'I don't know. Did you see how Magnus was waiting for something to happen? And it did!'

Cai shook his head. 'Do you think he wants Morcanta to rule? Maybe he even helped her find the torc! Where did she find it?'

'What is happening?' Brendan asked.

'Wait a moment!' I said quickly in Latin, then continued with Cai in our own tongue. 'Who knows? She will have to explain that to the Council. And I guess they will have to examine it, make sure it really is the neck-ring of our ancestors.'

'I don't think it can be; it looks too shiny and new!'

'Queen Aurelia's heavy gold necklace that she usually wears is very old, yet it always looks bright and new. Maybe gold doesn't age the way other things do.

'Let's go,' I added, noticing that most people were leaving. Morcanta was walking slowly with a haughty air, her friends close at her side to steady her. 'We still have to find Bem.'

'Bem!' Brendan had caught the last word. 'Does someone know where he is?'

Stinker gave a short bark and nuzzled his nose into Brendan's hand, then sat at his feet, gazing up and wagging his tail furiously.

'You want to find him too, don't you boy!' Cai reached over and scratched behind Stinker's huge ears.

'We are going to look for Bem,' I said to Brendan. 'Will you join us?'

Brendan's face fell. 'Abbot Feoras will expect me to return, as soon as the feast is over.'

He glanced over to the monks, who were waiting while Feoras had a word with Magnus.

Seeing the wise man gave me an idea.

'Wait for me.' I threaded my way through the crowd until I reached Magnus. He was just turning away when he saw me.

'Vibiana.'

He smiled, and I knew he thought I was going to launch into a thousand questions about Morcanta and the torc and the future of Caerleon. I would save those for later.

'Bem is missing. Do you have any idea where he might be?'

Magnus frowned. 'I had not heard this. Where was he last seen, and when?'

I told him everything we knew, which wasn't much.

'We've looked everywhere and asked everyone; no one has seen him since yesterday.'

'That in itself is very strange. Most people would say they saw him every single day. You are right to be worried.'

'What can we do? Can you help us find him?'

'Do you truly want my help?'

'Of course! We've told the Abbey, and they will pray.'

'Good.'

'But you have other means of knowing things.'

Magnus nodded, his dark eyes searching mine.

'So, maybe you could find out where Bem has gone. Either he is lying injured somewhere and we need to find him quickly, or—'

'Or he's somewhere quite safe, being looked after, but not able to make his way back to us.' Magnus was trying to make me feel better but it wasn't working.

'Don't forget, the last person to see him was Morcanta. She claims she sent him off on an errand.'

'At least I can find out from Morcanta where she sent him. That would be a place to start, before taking – other measures.'

'Using the glass globe.'

Magus gave a slight bow. 'You know everything, Vibiana.'

I doubted that. 'Can you see her tonight, now? If we just knew where to look –'

'All right, Vibiana, I will go to her now. If nothing else, she must answer questions about how the torc appeared so mysteriously, and just at the right time!' Magnus touched my arm briefly and left the room.

I ran back to Cai and Brendan and asked them to wait for me, then raced across the darkened courtyard after Magnus. I wanted to hear what Morcanta said to him if I could. The fact was I didn't trust Magnus completely. I couldn't help wondering if he had a part in the torc's sudden appearance.

As it happened, I couldn't get close enough to hear anything except a confused murmur. Morcanta's servants guarded her door and I didn't want to be seen lurking outside, so I drifted back and sat in the dark on the stone rim of the central pond. When I saw a glimpse of white in the doorway, I stood up.

'Magnus!' I whispered, as he drew near.

'You startled me! It is good I did not drop this in the dirt.' He held up something wrapped in a cloth.

'She gave you the torc?'

'I insisted on taking it away, for examination. I do not trust coincidences, especially ones which benefit the person to whom they happen.'

'How will you decide if it's the real one?'

'There are certain tests I can do. Unfortunately I don't have enough gold of equal weight, to try out Archimedes' theory! It does look real. The problem is, our ancestors did not keep written records. The one drawing we have was probably based on stories handed down for generations. This one does resemble the drawing: the thick circle of twisted gold, the end knobs in the shape of dragons.'

'I'd rather have Taran as ruler!'

'Yes,' he sighed. 'Can you imagine Morcanta uniting the people? She has so few supporters, I fear the kingdom will split into several parts and no one part will be strong enough to withstand the invaders.'

I walked beside him as he headed to his chamber, feeling relief wash over me. At least he agreed with us about Morcanta!

'Did she tell you anything about Bem?'

'She asked him to go into Caerleon town, to buy a special kind of honey she wanted.'

'Why didn't she just send a servant?'

'She claims she was helping Bem feel useful; that people treat him like an idiot, but he is really rather clever and just needs encouragement.'

That surprised me, for it was just what I thought myself. Tomorrow I would go to the shop that sold honey, ask if they'd seen Bem. We reached Magnus' chamber and went inside. I thought of something else.

'Where do the invaders come from, and what do they want here?'

'They come from across the southern sea. Who knows why? Perhaps they were driven out of their own lands, or simply want adventure. They march westward across Britain and may be crossing the Great River into our lands at this very moment. We must have a ruler who can unite our people. Even better if he can draw all the tribes of Cambria together. Then our army will be very strong.'

I wanted very much to watch Magnus examine the torc, but I couldn't hang around when Bem might be in danger. I said a quick goodnight and rushed back to the dining room. Cai was standing outside waiting for me, jumping up and down with impatience. Stinker leaped on me, nearly knocking me down.

'Where's Brendan?' I gave Stinker a shove and

he put his paws on the ground, contenting himself with licking my face with his rough tongue. 'Stop that!' I wiped the slobber with the hem of my tunic.

'You were so long! He had to leave – he didn't dare ask the abbot's permission to stay with us. And Arthur hasn't come back. Did you find out anything about the torc?'

I told Cai most of what Magnus had said.

'Invaders crossing the river!'

I nodded. 'What if Bem is out there somewhere, and they run across him? We must look for him!'

Every time Stinker heard Bem's name, he gave an excited bark and turned a circle.

'Bem will be safer in the dark on his own, than the two of us crashing around looking for him,' Cai said. 'Let's wait until tomorrow, when we can see. We'll get Arthur to help. Anyway, he'll be angry if we leave him out.'

I didn't want to wait, but Cai argued until I gave in. He was becoming more bossy than I was!

He left, pulling a reluctant Stinker with the rope, and I thought again of Magnus. I wanted to see what he had discovered about the torc, or if he had used the globe to find where Bem might be. But when I reached his chamber, the door and windows were shuttered tightly. I was sure he was awake but I didn't dare knock.

What was he doing that made him hide in secret behind a locked door? Whatever it was, it meant using his dark arts, and I was the one who told him to do it. I felt like I had jumped into the river and the waters were way over my head.

A Dangerous Mission

*There are times when you must
do a thing you know is dangerous,
if it might save someone else.*

'I'm not about to go into Druid Wood in the middle
of the night, even with the two of you!' Cai folded
his arms and stood his ground. 'You may be more
clever than me, but I think you're both mad!'

'Oh come on, Cai,' Arthur said impatiently.
'We'll never find Bem if we don't look where
Magnus said.'

That morning Magnus had sent for Cai and me.
Without giving anything away about his methods,
he had told us that Bem was probably still alive,
somewhere in Druid Wood. I wanted to ask him
about the torc but he'd looked exhausted and out
of sorts, so I decided to wait until we'd brought
Bem back safely.

'It isn't the middle of the night!'

I was trying to convince myself as much as Cai.
It was late afternoon on the day after the feast, and
the three of us were at our place by the rock on
the High Hill. Arthur had been with his father all
day, so we'd had to wait to set off looking for Bem.
I wondered if we shouldn't have just gone on our
own, as soon as Magnus told us.

'But it's nearly sundown! How can we "look"
as you put it, in the dark?'

'I've thought of that!' I said. 'See, I've brought

brushwood for torches. And a jar of goose fat in case we need to make more.'

'Oh, that will really be useful,' Cai said. 'We can rub it on our wounds if someone attacks us. Or some *thing*.'

'Do shut up, both of you!' Arthur snapped.

Cai and I stared at him. This wasn't like him at all. I guess losing the kingdom first to Taran and then to his step-sister, his father about to die, now Bem gone, was enough to put anyone out of sorts.

'Why don't we get Brendan to come with us?' I said.

'What good will that do?' Cai wanted to know.

'I just think we are going around in circles, and I don't trust Magnus as much as I used to. Brendan seems close to God. Maybe he can put in a special request for us.'

'Oh all right then,' Arthur said. He didn't seem to care much what we did.

'You two find Brendan while I go and make sure Zea is taken care of.' I handed Cai the torches and jar of fat.

'It will be dark before you return!' Cai shouted after me.

I just shook my head and started running down the hill to the villa. Although I'd been with Zea most the day, her colour hadn't been good and I wanted to be certain she was well looked after.

When I entered Zea's chamber the servant girl was kneeling by the wheelchair, patting her hand. Zea smiled to see me, but I could see from her face that she was in pain. I motioned to the girl to come outside.

'What's wrong?'

'I'm not sure.' The girl was only about ten but seemed wise and quick-witted for her age. 'I've sent for the doctor.'

'Good. If he's not here within the hour, send for Magnus. He'll know what to do.'

I went over and gave Zea a quick kiss.

'I must go on an important errand with Arthur, Grandmother. I won't be long.'

'Be careful, child.'

I tried to ignore how weak her voice sounded. I didn't want Zea to know Bem was missing, but she seemed to guess I might be in some danger. I certainly wasn't about to tell her we were headed into Druid Wood.

'Don't fret,' I said, gently squeezing her hand.

She nodded. 'I have always loved you like my own granddaughter, you know that.'

I nodded and hugged her tightly.

Her voice sounded even weaker as she whispered, 'The Lord will bless you. He will stay close to you, if you follow his way.'

'You know I love you, Grandmother,' I said. 'I'll come soon.'

As I was leaving I thought of a small dagger Arthur had given me ages ago, which I kept in the wooden chest. I took it out and stuck it through my belt, just in case. As I raced back up the hill, I tried to put Zea out of my mind. We had work to do; it wouldn't help to be distracted. I would come back the moment we had found Bem alive, or – no, I had to put that from my mind, as well.

'Here she is!' Cai shouted.

Brendan grinned and waved as I reached the rock, which had turned rose-coloured in the setting sun.

'Greetings, Little Sister,' he called in our own tongue.

I laughed, astonished. He spoke awkwardly, but I could easily understand him.

'You've been having lessons!'

'No, only listening. I cannot say much.

'But do not worry,' he added in Latin, 'now I can talk in both languages!'

The three of us groaned.

'Come on, let's be serious,' Arthur said. 'What's our plan?'

'I say we go around the wood,' Cai said. 'Bem probably went through and out the other side.'

I shook my head. 'You know we have to search the wood. That's where Magnus says he is.'

Arthur frowned. 'Yet Stinker led us to the riverside. Who told Magnus he was in the wood?'

'Uh, I'm not sure.' I thought Arthur or Brendan might refuse to go, if they knew we were depending on magic arts to find Bem.

'Whoever took Bem away,' Cai said, 'they could have used a boat, then put ashore downstream, carried him into the wood. It would have been a clever way to put Stinker off the scent.'

'I have brought coals in case we need to light torches,' Brendan said, holding up a small clay pot with holes. 'Abbot Feoras has given his blessing, and the monks will pray for us tonight.'

'Do we stay together, or split up?' I asked.

Arthur replied, 'Stay together at first. We can divide up later, but it must be well thought out. We don't want more people lost!'

We climbed the hill single file, following Arthur. At the wood's edge he paused and held up his hand.

'Brendan, say a prayer for us,' Arthur commanded. There was a fierceness in his voice now, and I was glad. This was more like the Arthur I knew!

We all knelt down, and Brendan spoke a prayer in the language of Hibernia, then repeated it for us in Latin.

'Oh Lord Christ, go with us into this dark wood. Darkness is as light to you, may your light shine on our path. By your strong Spirit, beat back the evil spirits which have been allowed to rule here. And dear Lord, please lead us to find your servant Bem.'

We knelt in quiet for a moment. I glanced at Cai. He lifted his chin as if ready to take on the forces of evil single-handed. I also felt a surge of courage.

'Let's go!' Arthur said.

We got to our feet and stepped forward into the gloom of Druid Wood.

We Need Light!

I am trying to get out of my mind
the smell of damp earth, the feeling
of being in a small enclosed place.

Under our feet the fallen leaves were like sunbursts of yellow and deep orange. It was hard for four people to walk without making noise. Still, we decided not to call out for Bem until we were sure no one else was in the wood. I told Arthur what Magnus had said about the invaders, but he said he'd known for a long time that barbarians were coming. The last of the sun winked behind us and slipped out of sight. The faces of my three friends seemed to float in the half-light under the close-knit trees. I shivered in spite of my warm cloak.

'Which way?' Arthur asked.

'I followed Morcanta and Bem into the wood once,' I whispered.

'You never said!' Arthur motioned for Cai and Brendan to stop.

'I didn't think it was important, but now I wonder. Morcanta was following Bem, so maybe this is a place he comes often.'

'Why would he do that?' Cai said.

'I don't know. There's an old stone altar, and some kind of large round hole filled with trees and bushes. Morcanta fell into it. Let's look there. If Bem is there, he may be stuck and not able to climb out.'

I took the lead, with Arthur right behind. Cai brought up the rear, translating for Brendan.

Before long, I couldn't see enough to put one foot in front of the other.

'We need light!' I whispered.

Brendan found a dry stick on the ground and held it to the coals in his pot. When it took fire, I handed each person a clump of beaten saplings soaked in fat and we lit our torches.

The tree trunks nearby leaped into view, the harsh light casting deep shadows on either side. I tried not to think of how easy it would be for anyone to see us, and also to hide from us, as we could only see what was directly in our circle of torchlight. A beetle scooted down from the flaming end of my torch and clung to the back of my hand until I flicked it off.

'This way.' I headed for a slight open space between the trees.

'Are you sure you know where you're going?' Cai asked.

'Yes!' Well, fairly sure. Of course, that had been in broad daylight, and now I remembered how I'd almost lost my way even then.

The torchlight seemed to light a fire under Brendan, and he began a long story in Latin, something about pigs and his many brothers and sisters and the village festival. We trudged on to the sound of Brendan's voice, picking our way through bushes and brambles.

'We're going in circles!' Cai complained after a while.

'No we're not! But maybe we aren't going as directly as we could be.'

'Stop a moment,' Arthur said.

We circled around him, our faces like leering masks in the harsh light. The smell of hot tree resin was strong in my nostrils.

'Brendan, what should we do?'

Brendan shook his head, his curls moving energetically. 'I am not the one to ask. I have no special knowledge, I am only a friend of the Lord Christ.'

'Then we must ask him again,' Arthur said.

We all knelt again, and again Brendan said a prayer. Cai and I were about to get to our feet, when suddenly Arthur spoke.

'Lord Christ, help us to find Bem! Please.'

'Amen,' the three of us murmured.

As we started off, I suddenly saw something pale up ahead.

'The stone! This way!' I led them quickly over to the old altar but as soon as my flare lit the grey surface of the stone, I stopped in my tracks.

'What is it, Vibiana?' Arthur nearly trod on my heel.

'Look!'

We held our torches high. The brambles which had covered the flat rock last time I was here had been cut back, and something lay on it. Something horrible. Arthur reached out and poked the charred object with his finger, and ashes fell away to reveal small bones.

'A vole,' he said. 'Or a small hare.'

Brendan and Cai had joined us by now.

'Someone is using this as a place of sacrifice,' I whispered.

'Who?' asked Cai. 'And why?'

I shook my head. I didn't know, didn't want even to think that it must be someone I knew, someone who lived in the villa. Who would come into Druid Wood, catch and kill an animal, burn it on the ancient stone?

'Let's move on,' Arthur said.

'Wait – this is near the place where Morcanta fell into a hole.'

I motioned them forward, stepping carefully to be certain of solid ground under my feet. Suddenly my foot thrust downward. I pulled it back, holding out my hand to warn the others.

'How broad is the hole?' Arthur asked. It was too dark to see the ring of trees around it.

'A bit smaller than the villa courtyard, I think.'

'Then we will split up, follow the edge of the hole two by two, meet on the other side.'

Brendan said, 'If Bem is here, we should call out for him. Bem!' he shouted, not waiting for us to agree. 'Bem, where are you?'

Arthur and Brendan went to the right and Cai came with me to the left as we walked around the edges of the hole. It was slow going. We were constantly shoving brambles aside or stepping heavily on them to weigh them down, each waiting so the thorny twigs didn't jump back and lash the other. At the same time we had to watch that we didn't step sideways and sink into the hole. Even with our torches it was hard to see where to put our feet.

'Bem!' I called softly. 'Bem, are you there?'

'Bem!' Cai called. 'Bem, answer us!'

We could hear Brendan and Arthur calling from

the other side. The bare trees seemed to catch our voices and toss them back to us. I found myself keeping in my head the image of Stinker stretched out contentedly by the fire. It was a picture of all that was wholesome and safe and good.

'You know,' Cai said after a time, 'this must be a sacred pond.'

'What do you mean?'

'This large round hole. Now, it's filled with small trees and undergrowth, but once there would have been water here.'

'Brendan said something about a pond in the wood. Oh, I know, he said the Druids would throw their treasures in the pond, as sacrifice to the gods.'

We walked on in silence for a while.

'Do you think—' I began.

'Do you reckon—' Cai said.

We halted and stared at each other. Cai's dark face under the torch was like the image of one of the old gods. I shuddered. Then he grinned, breaking the illusion.

'Vibiana, what if the torc was right here at the bottom of this pond!'

'And somehow Morcanta got Bem to find it for her!' I wasn't thinking any longer about keeping my voice down.

'What if she had to get rid of Bem, because he knew too much?'

We stared at each other.

Then the hairs stood up on the back of my neck, for I heard a sound. It came from somewhere nearby, a weird warbling noise like nothing animal or human.

I put my finger to my lips and motioned to Cai that we should douse our torches. He shook his head fiercely, but I ignored him and thrust my torch downward, kicking earth over the burning end and stamping on it until it went out. Cai muttered but finally did the same. I grasped the sleeve of his tunic with my hand, and we moved slowly towards where the sound had come from.

We heard it again. It sounded more human, like someone in pain.

'Bem!' I called.

The noise became louder, turned into a yelp that dissolved into a garbled cry of 'Vibiana!'

I pushed past Cai and crashed through the undergrowth to my left, away from the pond.

'Help me!' I called to Cai. I could hear him thrashing along behind me, cursing under his breath for not having the torch.

'Bem!'

'Here!' His voice was weak.

'Where? Ouch!'

I stamped my foot in frustration. He sounded so close but my hands ran into a thick wall of brambles. I heard him say something but I missed it, so I kept still for a moment and listened harder. I could just make out one word.

'Under.'

I fell on my knees and called again.

'Here.' Bem's voice sounded louder, as if our being there gave him strength.

I flipped my hood over my head and crawled under the thick bush towards the sound of his voice. Thorns plucked at my hands and clothing, but I kept going, calling all the time and always hearing a weak answer. Cai tried to follow me but I told him to wait. I wasn't sure where I was going and it was no use both of us getting wound up in brambles.

I stretched my hand out, feeling the way ahead, when suddenly a hand grabbed mine and squeezed.

'Bem!' I shouted. 'I've got him! Hold tight and I'll pull you out.'

'Can't. Bem tied up.'

I struggled the last few paces forward, my face nearly in the dirt. Then my head was free of the undergrowth, and I pulled myself out. I felt Bem's breath on my cheek.

'Ow!' I tried to stand but cracked my head on something hard. I put my hand up and touched solid rock, then explored a bit further and realised we were in a small cave or underhang from a rock.

'What's going on?' Cai called impatiently.

'It's a cave. Bem's all right, I think. Bem, are you hurt?'

Bem started to cry, but I thought it was more from happiness that he'd been found. He probably needed food and drink, if he'd been here the whole two days.

'I think he's all right. We'd better wait here for Arthur and Brendan. You stay there; there's not room here for three, and they will see you when they come with their torches.'

I heard him stamping around trying to find a stone or log to sit on. I huddled next to Bem. Now that I wasn't moving, the chill damp of the cave began to seep through my clothing. For a moment I felt panic at being closed in this small dark place.

'Vibiana.'

'Yes, I'm here.'

'Vibiana – knife?'

What an idiot I was! I took the dagger from my belt and felt around until my fingers touched rough hemp. I followed the rope one way and found it secured Bem's ankles; the other way reached to a ring of metal which had been hammered into solid rock.

'Keep very still.' I began to saw at the rope between his ankles.

'Who put you here?' The knife went back and forth with a squeaking sound.

'Lady will come for Bem.'

'Did Morcanta put you here?'

There was silence, during which he might have been shaking his head or nodding. 'Morcanta.'

I couldn't tell if he was agreeing with me, or simply repeating what I'd said. What was taking Arthur and Brendan so long? They should have reached us long before now in their circle of the pond. I wondered if I was losing track of time.

At last the ropes fell loose.

'You're free. We'll wait for Arthur to come with his torch.'

But Arthur and Brendan never came. Overcome by the cold and lateness of the hour, I dozed off.

When I awoke, my mouth was parched and my body was stiff all over. I sat up and rubbed my eyes, looking down at Bem who was asleep. I could see him quite clearly in the grey light.

Fear squeezed at my throat. It was dawn. What had happened to Arthur?

Invaders in Druid Wood

The barbarians are people, as we are.
They have wives and children,
they eat, drink and make jokes.
Still, they have no right to take our kingdom from us!

'Cai!' I whispered loudly.

Nothing. I called his name again, this time in a normal voice.

'Whu-ah–'

I heard shuffling and rustling as Cai shifted and woke.

'Ugnh!'

'Wake up! What's happened to Arthur?'

There was silence as Cai took this in.

'I haven't seen anything! I fell asleep and ended up stuck behind this log. Zeus, it's cold! Can you get Bem out?'

'If you help me.'

I nudged Bem awake. In the dim light I saw a jug; it held water. I gave it to Bem and he drank eagerly. At least whoever put him here hadn't wanted him to die.

Now we could see what we were doing, it wasn't so hard to find a way out. Cai got a dead branch and held back the brambles. I crawled out first, then helped pull Bem through without too many scratches. He was smudged all over with dirt and I guessed I looked the same.

'Stinker?' Bem asked.

'He's fine. We had to leave him behind because

he's so noisy! I've put one of the boys in charge of him.'

'Arthur's missing,' Cai said. 'And Brendan.'

'Let's start back. Maybe they got lost and went back home already. If not, we can send out searchers.'

Small birds chirped and scampered from limb to limb in the bare trees, as we made our way back towards the old altar stone. I felt numb, relieved we had found Bem but trying not to panic about Arthur. I couldn't imagine him giving up and going home. He knew where we would be, and the round pond made it hard to lose one's way.

Unless they fell in!

'Cai, what if Arthur and Brendan fell into the hole?'

'We'd have heard them cry out, wouldn't we?'

'Arthur!' I shouted, hearing my voice come back at me from the other side of the pond. 'Brendan!'

'Here we are!'

Cai and I ran forward, leaving Bem to catch up as best he could. Arthur and Brendan stepped out from behind a massive oak just beyond the altar.

'Were you hiding from us?' I was about to scold them, when I saw their faces more clearly and stopped. 'What happened?'

'We'll tell you on the way. Bem!' Arthur said, clapping him on the back. 'You found him! Where was he?'

As we made our way quickly out of the wood, Cai and I told them about the cave behind the brambles. 'We're not sure who put him there – it might have been Morcanta. But where were you?'

Arthur and Brendan looked at each other.

'With the barbarians,' Arthur said.

'The barbarians! Where were they? Did they capture you? Why did they let you go? Are they following us?'

'One question at a time, Little Sister!

'It was like this: once we were well on the other side of the pond, we heard a noise and thought it might be Bem. But then, as we followed the sound, we could tell it was a campsite with a large number of people. Then we saw the light of their fire. I thought it might be invaders, so we were careful to go slowly and make no noise.'

Brendan said, 'All of a sudden, someone grabbed us!'

'Yes, there were watchmen in the trees. They tied our hands behind our backs, took us to their camp. I wish you could have seen it! So many men, women, children, all very rough looking with wild hair, wearing bright-coloured cloaks. They had their weapons to hand in case of need: I saw lots of spears and some axes, hardly any swords though. And very few horses.'

'And when they spoke, it sounded like this!' Brendan made gargling noises deep in his throat.

'How did you get away?' Cai asked.

'We didn't. They let us go.'

'Why would they do that?' I asked.

'I'm not sure,' Arthur said. 'They obviously didn't think we were worth killing. They poked at us and ran their hands through our hair and pulled at our tunics, things like that.'

'They laughed very much!' Brendan said. 'I sang for them, they were pleased and clapped.'

'Yes, that may have saved us,' Arthur said, smiling at Brendan. 'Their chieftain – a man broad as an oak door, he was the one they deferred to – he made Brendan sing another time, then he gave an order and two men with spears led us back into the forest.'

'I thought they would kill us then!' Brendan said. 'I fell on my knees and began to pray, to make myself ready to die and meet my Lord face to face.'

'I thought the same, but the men just laughed and one of them prodded Brendan to his feet with the blunt end of his spear. Then they turned back and left us there.'

'What was the point?' I wondered. 'Now, you will go back and tell everyone, and the invaders can't surprise us!'

We reached the edge of the wood. The sun was rising behind us, bathing the meadow below with a sudden glow. The kingdom of Caerleon spread out below us.

'That was exactly the point, I think,' Arthur said as we stood still for a moment, taking in the welcome scene of our homeland. 'They want us to be warned. They are not at all afraid of us. Perhaps they will feel their victory is even greater, if we are prepared for them and are still conquered.'

'What will we do?' Cai asked.

'I don't know yet.' Arthur turned to us, and the look in his hazel eyes was sharp enough to split rocks. 'But one thing I do know: I'm not going to let it happen!'

A Torc of Pure Gold

*The evil one has been so very
cunning, but she has not reckoned
with the cleverness of Arthur!*

I raced over the rough grass down the hill to the villa, not looking back, picking up speed until I felt I was flying. All I could think of was warning the warriors, getting them ready in case the invaders were on our heels. Then I would go straight to Morcanta.

'Caradoc! Rhys!'

I called out for the warlords as I stumbled into the barracks yard, completely out of breath. A couple of warriors heard me and ran to get their leaders.

'Arthur,' I gasped as Caradoc grabbed my arm, trying to make sense of my panted words. 'Barbarians – Druid Wood!'

That was enough. Caradoc nodded fiercely and soon the war-house was filled with shouting and crashing.

'What's going on?' Arthur demanded, arriving just then with Cai.

'I told them the invaders were coming.'

He frowned at me. 'Don't be so hasty! You should have waited for me.'

'I was only trying to help!'

Arthur ran inside the barracks and Cai followed him. I felt my face hot with shame. I hadn't thought. I guess he felt like I was trying to take over instead of letting him lead.

Women weren't allowed in the warriors' living quarters but I got as near the door as I dared. I could hear Arthur yelling above the din.

'The barbarians are camped in Druid Wood, but they won't attack yet. We have time to prepare. They'll wait at least until sundown, probably several days.'

There was a confused roar as the men shouted their questions.

'I know this because they captured me, and Brendan. They seemed relaxed and settled, not like men on the brink of war. They didn't know who I was, and they let us go.'

'Are you so sure of that, *Prince* Arthur?' I recognised Taran's voice.

'Yes, I am sure! They are over-confident – they want to conquer us in spite of our being warned. If we plan well and don't lose our heads, we can win against them.'

'Who will lead our men? They won't be led by a woman, even one with a gold ring around her neck. Am I right, lads?'

Shouts of approval at this.

'Or a servant girl!' one man called, and the others broke out laughing. I wished I could turn into a bug and crawl under the water trough.

'I will lead you,' Arthur said. His voice sounded calm and steady. 'Prepare your weapons and your horses. Make sure everything is ready, and stay alert. We'll meet again at sundown.'

More shouting, some protesting that Taran was their leader. I moved away from the door as several men darted out and headed for the stables. Arthur appeared in the doorway.

'Where are you going?'

'To my step-sister.' His face was like rain-clouds.

'I'm coming with you!'

He shook his head but then shrugged. 'Try to keep a bridle on your tongue.'

Cai dashed off to the armoury and I joined Arthur, nearly running to keep up with his determined strides. I could tell he was still put out with me so I kept quiet.

In the main courtyard Bem was laughing and clapping as Brendan threw a stick to Stinker. The large hairy dog twirled in mid-air, snatched the stick and raced to Bem with it. Bem grabbed the stick and Stinker barked and leaped with mad joy.

As we neared Morcanta's quarters, we encountered Magnus.

'Wait.' I put a hand on Arthur's arm. 'Magnus was going to test the torc, see if it was genuine.'

'Greetings, Arthur and Vibiana.' The teacher raised his thick eyebrows. 'You both look as if a bath would be a good idea.'

'We found Bem!' I said.

'So I see. And was he where I told you he would be?' Magnus smiled knowingly.

'Yes, he was. But – we all prayed about it as well, and the Abbey was praying.'

'Ah. So you wonder, what is the source of your help. Does it really matter? You found him, if by one means or another, or both, that is not so important.'

I nodded but his answer didn't satisfy me. I would think on it further when I had the chance. Arthur cut in impatiently.

'Magnus, what have you learned about the torc Morcanta wears?'

'I have tested it carefully. As far as I can tell, it is pure gold.'

'Oh,' we both said. That was it then. How could Arthur hope to lead the people now? Would the Council change their minds?

Magnus wagged his finger at us. 'However – I also discovered fine grains of sand in the grooves of the knobs. Not visible to the eye, but only in the brightest light, under my magnifying lens.'

'Which means what?' Arthur asked.

'That sand is not the kind found on the banks of the river, or in any other place in Caerleon. It is something I import specially for my laboratory, to use in dousing fires or various arts of metal. It is the kind used in casting gold.'

'You think someone here made the torc, here, and recently!'

'It appears so. Damp sand is used to make a mould for the gold knobs to be cast in. As the sand came from my workroom, suspicion rests on Gruffin. He has been taken to prison in Caerleon town, and I have just now informed Morcanta. If you are going to see her, be aware that her mood at the moment is somewhat fragile!'

'Why has she not been arrested?' Arthur demanded.

'She protests her innocence. Gruffin brought her the torc so she says, and he agrees, although he's vague as to where he found it. As long as they tell the same story, there's nothing to be done but punish him.

'There is something else,' he went on. Go and examine the torc for yourselves, see what you make of it.'

As Magnus left us I whispered to Arthur, 'Gruffin is probably terrified what Morcanta would do to him, if he said she had any part in this!'

'Let's see if she will be more forthcoming about Bem.'

We stopped by the central pond and scrubbed our faces and hands as best we could. I tried to slick down my hair but I could feel it spring back as soon as I pressed on it.

Morcanta's servant girl didn't want to let us in. 'My mistress is fatigued –'

'Let them enter!' Morcanta didn't sound tired to me.

'Step-brother, yes, what is it?'

She flicked her eyes up and down at his dirty tunic, but didn't even glance at me once. Morcanta reclined on her couch, her hair spread out in a fan of reddish gold. The torc lay on a scrap of blue linen on the low table in front of her. Various women lurked nearby, but they disappeared at a commanding clap from Morcanta.

'Norwenna, stay.'

The pock-marked woman moved to the doorway and stood like a statue.

Arthur didn't try to be polite. 'I know you tried to force your way into the kingship with a false torc.'

'You're uninformed. Gruffin offered me this, saying he had found it.'

'Did he say where?'

'No.'

'Or perhaps you paid him to make it for you.'

'Perhaps.' Her lips curled in what might have been a smile, except it looked like a sneer coming from her. 'Perhaps not. Gruffin says not.'

'Of course!' I burst out. 'You've probably threatened to have him cut to pieces if he said anything else!'

Still Morcanta refused to acknowledge I was even in the room.

'Magnus went on and on about the kind of sand he found on it,' Morcanta said, 'but that could come from anywhere – Gruffin could have hidden it in Magnus' workroom. There's sand all over the place there!'

'That's not why I've come,' Arthur said.

At this Morcanta sat up and clapped her hands again. As if by magic, three women appeared and she made a few swift hand signals. They nodded: one left and returned with three silver goblets of wine and a small plate of sugared dates. The other two joined Norwenna by the door as if to guard our escape, or at least to listen to every word said.

'Sit. Please.'

She waved us to a low couch opposite. So, I was to be allowed to sit and drink wine also!

'Drink,' Morcanta urged, but Arthur shook his head.

'Someone took Bem into Druid Wood, chained him up in a cave and left him.'

'So, you have found him! That is good.' Morcanta hid her face for a moment as she lifted the goblet with both hands and drank deeply.

'What do you know of this?' Arthur asked, signalling me with a slight motion of his hand to keep quiet.

'Nothing. I am sorry someone would treat a simple person so ill. As I told Magnus, I sent him into Caerleon to buy honey. It's hardly my fault if he was attacked on the way.'

'He told me he was waiting for the "Lady" and I'm sure that meant you!'

Arthur gave me a stern look but didn't interrupt.

'He is fond of me; I cannot help that. I enjoy having him come and sing to me.'

At last Morcanta admitted my existence! I pressed my advantage.

'You thought he could tell you where to find the *real* torc.'

Her white face flushed with a tinge of red. It came and went in an instant, but I knew I'd hit on the truth.

Arthur leaned forward. 'Or maybe you thought you could hold him to ransom. In case your trick with the false torc didn't work, you would offer an exchange: Bem's life, for the kingdom.'

'How very shrewd. I wish I had thought of that myself.'

Morcanta took the torc from the table.

'This is absurd! I had no need to look further, or hold Bem to ransom! Magnus is mistaken. This is the ancient torc. See, here is the dragon symbol, just as in the old drawing.'

Arthur took the heavy circlet of gold from her hand. Together, we eyed it closely.

'Hmm.' He ran his finger over the dragon on

159

one of the gold knobs. 'Yes, it does look exactly like the drawing.' He placed the torc carefully back on the blue cloth.

'Come, Vibiana.'

Arthur stood quickly and bowed to Morcanta, and was out the door. I followed as gracefully as I could. Morcanta sat in frozen silence. Obviously she was as puzzled as I was, by our sudden exit.

Bem's Secret Place

*I always knew there was
much more in the mind of
Bem than he ever showed.*

'That torc!' Arthur said, as soon as we were out of Morcanta's hearing.

'What about it?'

'Remember the drawing we found, of the ancient torc? On the drawing, the dragons are sketchy, not drawn carefully and exactly. On the real torc, they would be well-formed, perhaps even filled with coloured stones. On Morcanta's, the dragons are clumsy. They look more like dogs. This torc is an exact copy – of an inexact drawing!'

'That settles it! Morcanta should have known better, but she was in a hurry – she wanted to shock us with her announcement at the feast.'

'How would they copy the drawing if you still have it?' I added.

'I don't. I didn't think anything of it, but it disappeared from my chamber soon after I showed it to you.'

'What now?'

Arthur's step slowed and he shook his head. 'I'm not sure. The best I can do is try to take control of the warriors, lead them in the attack against the barbarians.'

'Attack? Don't you mean defence?'

Arthur grinned at that. 'No, I mean attack. I have

an idea. It will take careful planning and timing, and everyone will have to work together.'

'Even Taran?'

'Especially Taran. If I can just win the warriors' trust –'

'I think you have done, for the most part.'

'That's not enough.' Arthur quickened his pace, heading for Magnus' workroom. 'I'm going to talk it all through with Magnus. He's the wisest person in all Caerleon, he'll help me see where the gaps are and how to bring all the people into agreement with the plan. Are you coming?'

'No. I have an idea of my own. I'll see you there later.'

'Stinker! Catch!'

Brendan tossed the stick at Stinker, who grabbed it in his mouth and then dropped it, panting. He flopped down into the hard dirt of the courtyard, ready to end the game. He wasn't a young dog any longer.

'Bem! Brendan! Come here a moment, I have something to ask you.'

Bem scuttled over in his lopsided gait, his face beaming. He was still dirty from his days in the cave but otherwise you wouldn't know anything had happened to him. Being reunited with his close companion was as good as medicine.

'Have you eaten?' I asked them.

Brendan nodded. 'The kitchen girls seemed bent on stuffing us like geese to be roasted!

'Now that you are here,' he added, 'I must go back to the Abbey.'

'Wait a moment. Look, both of you wash your faces, and follow me.'

Brendan led Bem over to the pond and helped him wash, while Stinker leaped full in and had a good noisy frolic.

When they were at least cleaner than when they started, and Stinker had splattered water all over us to his heart's content, I took them to Zea's chamber. I wanted to see how she was, and I didn't know any other place to have a quiet unobserved conversation.

'Stay there!' Bem ordered. Stinker immediately dropped on his haunches just outside Zea's doorway.

'How is my grandmother today?' I asked the servant girl. I didn't see Zea.

'She is sleeping now, but rests well. I gave her medicine in the night for her coughing, and it helped. I think she is no better, but no worse.'

'You're free to go, for the moment. I will sit here with my friends and look in on her. Stay in the courtyard or kitchen— I'll call if you're needed.'

The small girl smiled her thanks and slipped from the room.

After I peeked behind the curtain to satisfy myself Zea was breathing normally, I joined the others. Brendan and Bem sat on the low couch and I took a basket chair.

'Will you try something for me?' I asked Brendan.

'Of course.'

'It may sound foolish, but I believe Bem knows something about the torc.'

Bem smiled and nodded, but that meant

163

nothing, as we were speaking in Latin. He did that whenever he was spoken to.

'It is because of a song he sang once. He makes up beautiful songs that sound like poetry, and I think he could sing to us about what he knows, even if he cannot exactly say it.' I paused, wondering how to make this clear to Brendan.

'I understand! You want me to sing a question to Bem, and perhaps he will sing the answer for us.'

'Yes!' I was amazed he'd caught on so quickly. 'I want you to ask him if he knows where the golden torc can be found.'

'It is only, I must sing in your language, I am not sure of the words.'

'I will help you.'

We thought out what words Brendan would use while Bem looked on, humming to himself. Then Brendan began to hum as well, trying out various tunes. All this took a very long time.

'All right,' Brendan said finally. 'I am ready.'

He began to sing a jaunty tune, and Bem kept time by tapping his palm on his knee. It sounded like a real song, even if the words weren't exactly poetic:

> *O Bem dear friend,*
> *we must depend on you*
> *to show us where to go.*
> *The ancient golden neck-ring*
> *lost so long ago*
> *we now would find.*
> *Does Bem know?*

> *Lead us to the secret place of the golden ring,*
> *for only with the golden torc*
> *can Arthur be our king.*

Bem laughed and clapped his hands.

'Shush! Think of Zea! That was excellent, Brendan.'

Bem sat smiling and nodding, but didn't seem inclined to sing a reply.

'Bem?' I gave him a questioning look.

'Vibiana said shush.'

'It's all right — you may sing, just not too loudly.'

He nodded, then began to sing as if he'd been practising it for weeks. The tune included hints of Brendan's but with intricate variations.

> *Bem found the golden ring*
> *in an olden pond,*
> *with trees ringed round.*
> *He took the gold from the ground,*
> *to a secret place in the ancient wood.*
> *For Arthur's need, Bem will*
> *gladly give the ring.*
> *Arthur and none other must be king!*

Almost without a pause, Brendan sang:

> *Where is this secret place?*
> *Will Bem take his friends to the secret place*
> *where the neck-ring hides?*

Bem bent his head up and down several times.

'Quickly then!' I stepped to the doorway and

called for the servant, who came right away. Then I slipped behind the curtain to give Zea a kiss before leaving.

As we crossed the courtyard, it was obvious something was in the air. Servants darted from one chamber to another, calling out excitedly to each other. I heard shouting from the direction of the war-house. Justus strode past with several servants bounding behind him like eager puppies.

I put a hand on Bem's arm.

'Something is happening. We will go first to find Arthur.'

Preparing for War

*Caerleon preparing for war, the villa on the
move. Everywhere I look is confusion, yet there
is order in it, because Arthur has planned it well.*

'Why won't you tell me what's going on?' I
shouted, stamping my foot.

'You'll see soon enough, Little Sister.'

Arthur had to speak right in my face for me to
hear over the rapid clangs of metal on metal. He
smiled briefly at me, then turned to speak to the
head blacksmith.

Bem and Brendan waited for me outside the
blacksmith's. Inside, it was hotter than the middle
of summer. There were several fires blazing in the
large open shed, and the place was crowded with
sweaty men pounding sheets of metal with
hammers. I peered through the smoky gloom,
trying to make out what kind of swords or spears
they were crafting, but I couldn't tell.

I tugged on Arthur's sleeve. 'What are they
making?'

'Trumpets.'

'Trumpets?' Our warriors faced the biggest battle of
their lives, and the blacksmith was making trumpets?

I left in disgust, motioning for Brendan and Bem
to follow.

'What is happening?' Brendan asked.

'They are preparing for battle, but Arthur won't
say more. He's being very secretive!' I frowned and
kicked at a clod of dirt.

'And, they're making *trumpets.*'

Brendan leaned his head to one side in a thoughtful way.

'There are stories in the Holy Scriptures about battles with trumpets.'

'It doesn't matter. We need to find the real torc, so Arthur can be proclaimed king before the battle begins.'

We passed the carpenter's shed. Here at least, I knew what was happening. The making of bows and arrows had gone on for some time now, to be ready for any attack.

Workers were shaving long slender pieces of yew wood and rubbing them smooth. The finished articles were lined up neatly along the outer wall, and I stopped to pick one up. It was longer than my arm and delicately curved. I grasped the two slender ends and pulled. The wood bowed gently, as if made of river grass.

A murmur of delight escaped my lips. This was the finest bow I had ever seen. I hoped I would be using one of these in the battle. Then I felt a shiver down my spine. It would be a very different thing to shooting an arrow at a straw target. To shoot at a man, possibly to kill him— could I do that? Suddenly I saw in my mind a rough invader, wounded by my arrow in his chest, his wife and children waiting in vain for him to return. I wished my mind didn't play those tricks!

'Very beautiful,' said Brendan, 'but it will take from someone the life God has given.'

How did he read my thoughts! I sighed and let and my gaze travel over to another workshop, where a potter and his apprentice were turning out enough simple clay pots to serve every kitchen in the whole of Caerleon. Suddenly there was a rumble of wheels over hard dirt, and several men crossed the yard pulling brightly painted wheelchairs. Cai led the way, directing them.

My mouth dropped open.

'Chariots!' Bem said.

Of course! I only thought of wheelchairs because of Zea. Our people had used chariots even before the Romans and a number of the old ones were kept in constant readiness. They were like small platforms on wheels, designed to hold two men. The rawhide platforms swayed slightly, suspended from ropes attached to the frame. Incredibly light and fast, chariots would give us a big advantage over warriors on foot. Arthur said he hadn't seen many horses in the enemy camp.

As Cai passed us I called, 'Bem's found the lost torc and he's going to show us where it is!'

Cai nodded vaguely in my direction. 'This way!' he called to the men pulling the chariots.

'They do not even care about the torc!' I exclaimed. 'With Cai and Arthur, they think only of getting ready for battle. They do not consider the future— what will happen afterwards.'

'They focus on the task at hand, and have no time for anything else. We must be patient with them,' Brendan said.

'If they refuse to help, will you come with Bem and me to find the torc?'

'Only if Abbot Feoras says I may. Come with me now to the Abbey, I will ask him.'

I didn't want to go there again. I didn't want

to have to speak to Llian, but if I saw her I couldn't avoid it. Better not to go there at all!

'Oh, all right.' Maybe I could just wait outside the gate with Bem.

But when we reached the Abbey compound, the first person I saw was Llian. She was leading a loaded cart drawn by a donkey, coming out the gate as we were going in.

'What has happened?' Brendan asked.

As soon as he said that, I noticed the Abbey was bustling like an ant-hill stirred with a stick. Instead of the usual quiet orderly activity, all was movement. Voices called out hastily in a way I'd never heard there.

'Vibiana!' Llian seemed distracted.

'What is it, uh, Mother?'

'She is your mother?' Brendan's grey eyes looked like they would fall out of his head.

I nodded. 'What's wrong?'

'Have you not heard?' Llian's gentle face was puckered with anxiety. 'Arthur sent word that we must depart the Abbey, at once! Barbarians have entered Druid Wood and are preparing to attack us. We would be first in their way, so we must leave.'

'Where will you go?'

'Abbess Brangwen will tell us. We are to head downhill and gather near the bridge. There must be some plan to camp across the river. Did you come for me?'

'We want Abbot Feoras. Bem knows where the— where something is that's very important to Arthur. I need Brendan to come with me, to speak with Bem.'

Llian nodded, obviously not understanding. She didn't bother to ask questions.

'He and his men are in the chapel, praying for Caerleon in this time of crisis.'

We thanked her and hurried through the gate.

'Oh, Vibiana,' she called after us, 'wait a moment!'

I turned back and motioned for the others to go on.

Llian asked one of the men from the Abbey to take her place with the cart, and she led me a few paces aside.

'There's something I must say,' she began.

I stared down at my feet and held my breath. I hoped she wasn't going to complain about my ignoring her. I wouldn't have an answer, if she did. But I was surprised.

'I must ask you to forgive me.'

I raised my head and stared at her. Suddenly I realised that I was looking her straight in the eye. Here I was, already as tall as my mother yet feeling like a small irritable child.

'You aren't the one needing forgiveness.'

'Oh yes! I did not see it until Abbess Brangwen pointed it out to me after you were here the other day. But now I do. I have left you to grow up on your own! At the time, after the death of your father – well, I could do nothing but cry. They took me in here, comforted me, gave me simple tasks and taught me to pray – they helped me go on living. I thought I could serve you best by praying for you. But now I realise, it is time to move on. When this crisis is over, I want us to be together again, as we used to be.'

I looked away, not sure of what to say.

'I must go,' she added, 'but I'll see you soon. And promise me you won't go into the wood!'

I gave her a little wave and walked quickly on. There was so much to think out. Sometimes change was hard, even when it was for the better! I wasn't used to having a mother. Good thing she hadn't asked me to say I forgave her. I wasn't ready to do that just yet.

As for not going into the wood again, I didn't want to promise, because it was fairly clear from Bem's song that his 'secret place' was in Druid Wood. If the torc was there, that was where we would go, invaders or not.

A New Age

*We have come to the end
of a long journey.
A new age has begun!*

It took no time at all to find the Abbot. Brendan explained it all in his own language, and the Abbot asked many questions. Finally he nodded his approval.

'God go with you, my children!'

Feoras stood outside the chapel, tall and sombre in his brown robes. He lifted his hand in blessing.

'Go quickly! We will stay here and pray until you return safely.'

When we left the Abbey gate Bem turned up the hill and beckoned us on with a smile, humming under his breath. It was as I thought: Druid Wood was our destination.

Why was I less afraid to enter the gloomy forest this time? Maybe the thought of a flesh and blood enemy was less frightening than the idea of the old gods and spirits who might haunt this place. At least barbarians were real people, could be seen and heard.

Before we stepped under the towering trees I stopped and whispered, 'We must go quietly. No singing or talking, be very careful where you step. Do you both understand, the barbarians are here?'

They nodded, Bem with a carefree smile and Brendan deeply serious. I hoped Bem really did understand and wasn't agreeing just to please me.

'This way!' Bem said in a loud whisper.

I put my finger to my lips in warning. He grinned and motioned us on.

We took the same way as the day before, past the old altar. I tensed, waiting to see which direction we'd take around the hidden pond, then relaxed slightly as we turned to the left, towards the cave where we'd found Bem. At least we weren't heading right into the invader's camp, unless they had moved. Twice I heard something rustling behind us but when we stopped and listened, the noise ceased. It must have been a small animal, frightened into stillness.

With the occasional crunch of leaves underfoot, the three of us moved forward until we were right in front of the brambles hiding the entrance to the cave. There Bem halted, motioning downward with his hand as if to say we should crawl under.

'Bem!' I whispered. 'Are you telling us the torc is hidden in the cave where I found you?'

Bem's eyes lit up. 'Vibiana knows!'

'Then why did you not bring it with you when we were there?'

Bem shrank back from me and his face fell.

'Don't be unhappy,' I said quickly, as Brendan shook his head at me in a disappointed way. 'I'm not angry with you, Bem. I just don't understand.'

'Bem—bad women, safe for Arthur—special hiding place—' Bem stopped. He couldn't explain it clearly, but I guessed Morcanta's women had seen Bem crawl into the cave and decided to use it to imprison him. They would be furious when they learned how close they were to the real torc!

'Do not worry,' Brendan said, touching his arm gently. 'God has used you to keep the necklace safe. We will take it back to Caerleon and Arthur will be king.'

Bem's smiled and wiped his nose with the back of his hand.

'You wait here,' Brendan added. 'I will go.'

Again Bem made a downward motion with his hands, then curved his hand up and apparently plucked something from a high shelf. Brendan nodded and pulled up his cowl, crouching down under the brambles.

While we waited, hearing Brendan grunting as he crawled under the bushes, I asked, 'Where did Bem find the necklace?'

'I show you!'

He grabbed my arm and dragged me over to the edge of the pond. Although it was filled with trees, I knew it was a deep hole.

'Careful!'

'Safe.'

Bem pointed. I looked down and saw a depression at the edge of the pond, almost like a track leading down into the hole. I guessed it would be possible to slide down and then use the undergrowth to pull yourself out again.

'You found the torc in the pond?'

Bem nodded. So it was the Druids! They had thrown it into the pond long ago, when it held water. It must have been a sacrifice, to keep the gods of the wood happy.

'I have it!'

Snuffling like a rooting pig, Brendan crawled out

from under the brambles, a dirty bit of sacking cloth in one hand. He scrambled to his feet, holding it out to Bem. Bem took it gently, placed it in my hand like a delicate flower whose petals might fall. I didn't realise how heavy it was and almost dropped it at first. I wanted to rip the cloth but forced myself to unwrap it slowly. I pulled the last of the sacking away, and there it was.

We stared at the bright thing I held in both hands.

'It's nothing like the fake one.'

'Meant for a king,' Brendan said.

'Arthur.' Bem reached up one hand and stroked it gently.

The golden torc, the ancient neck-ring of our ancestors, was thicker than the one worn by Morcanta. Many strands of pure gold had been twisted together, to the thickness of a baby's arm. The knob-like ends which would fit under the throat were fighting dragons, and the dragon's eyes were set with deep red stones. Truly, it was fit for a king. I gazed at the royal necklace and felt that something important had concluded. What we sought for so long was found! Now the rule of Arthur could begin.

Coronation and Capture

*My head still hurts. When I think
of that woman I get so angry,
and my head hurts even more.*

In the event, Arthur's coronation was nothing like
I expected.

Across the river stood the old Roman
amphitheatre, just a large circle in the earth
surrounded by grassy banks. It hadn't been used in
a hundred years for anything other than a place to
hold the town festival.

Now the field was covered with tents and wattle
pens for livestock, soaking in the rains which had
come again. The whole villa, plus those from the
Abbey, had moved here! It was part of Arthur's
plan to fool the barbarians. I couldn't get close
enough to him to ask what he had in mind. He was
always surrounded by warriors coming to him for
orders. I could tell I'd just be in the way.

Magnus must know what was going on. I had
watched out for him and grabbed him as soon as I got
Zea settled. She was carried across the river in a covered
cart, with as much straw beneath her bed as I could
manage to claim from Justus. I sat by her and held her
hand as we jostled the short way down the hill. Rain
dripped onto the wooden cart roof. Even this short
journey could do her no good, and I hated for her to
leave her heated chamber. At least she and the king
were going to lodge at the doctor's house, where they
would be dry and have help if they needed.

'Please, God,' I muttered under my breath. I didn't know what to pray, just hoped he would hear and sort it out. Zea's eyes were closed, her faced pinched and pale.

Brendan lifted a hand in greeting as he marched by with the twelve men of Hibernia. Stinker trotted along at his heels.

'Where is Bem?'

'I do not know. Stinker could not find him either, so I told him to come with me, that we will find Bem later.'

That didn't surprise me, that Brendan could have a sensible conversation with a dog. But where was Bem? I felt uneasy but there was enough to worry about with getting Zea settled.

'Do you know what's happening? I can't get to Arthur to ask him.'

Brendan shook his head. 'Only that the invaders have moved from Druid Wood where Arthur and I saw them. Some say they are camped just over the western hill.'

We followed the king's cart through the narrow muddy streets of Caerleon town. The wooden houses were mostly one-storey, thatched with straw. Only the doctor's and a few of the wealthy were on two levels.

Julia greeted us at the door, glowing with excitement. She and her mother showed us two small but clean rooms at the rear on the ground floor. There was only a curtain between them. After the king was settled the men came back and carried Zea inside. I could hear a constant murmur on the other side of the curtain. It was the queen praying beside her dying husband. How could she stand it? His violent coughs made me want to cover my ears.

A small portable charcoal brazier gave plenty of warmth. Although there was little smoke, I asked Julia to have it moved for the moment, as I thought Zea might have trouble breathing. As I was smoothing Zea's coverlet, she reached one hand out and grabbed my wrist. I was startled at her sudden strength but it left as quickly as it came.

'What is it, Grandmother?' I took her hand gently in mine.

She seemed to be concentrating hard on what to say, and her lip trembled.

'It's all right, rest now.'

'No. First this: tell Magnus. Very important. You must be one or the other, not both. Not all things, but one thing. The best thing.'

My heart sank. I thought her mind was starting to wander.

'Tell him!'

'I will tell him, don't worry! Rest now.'

She sighed gratefully and let her eyes close.

After making sure all was in order, I left Zea with the faithful servant girl. I kissed her goodbye as I always did and she opened her eyes and smiled to reassure me she'd be all right.

I found Magnus at the ruined theatre.

'Just the person I want,' he said before I could get a word out. 'Run, ask the queen to join us in Arthur's tent.'

'What for?' I asked, but I spoke to the misty air. I ran quickly all the way back to the house I had just come from.

Queen Aurelia did not ask why she was summoned, but rose from the low stool at her husband's bedside with a dignified air, leaving him in care of a nurse. I tried to think of something to say as we walked towards the centre of the amphitheatre, where Arthur had his tent.

'Now we've found the torc, Arthur can be recognised as ruler of Caerleon,' I said finally.

The queen turned to me and smiled. I had never seen her eyes light up like that, and it made her suddenly beautiful. In the next instant the smile was gone and she gazed earnestly at me. We both had our hoods up to keep out the wet and she clutched my arm to make sure I was paying attention.

'Pray for him, Vibiana. This is the time of greatest danger. He will be ruler in name only until he proves himself.'

'I will,' I said, only it came out as a croak. I wished she hadn't entrusted any kind of praying to me! All I knew to do was look helplessly to God. Maybe that was enough, I didn't know.

It was a small tent, made smaller by the handful of people crowded into it. There was just about room for us to stand and not be hit by the long sword Rhys carried. Again Caliburn waited, this time to go to its rightful owner!

The queen sat on a low stool next to Arthur, who was flanked by Magnus and Caradoc. All three men – I was now thinking of Arthur as a man, not a boy – looked solemn, even grim. This should have been a celebration held in sunlight in sight of all Caerleon, but war changes everything. Two small round tables held oil lamps. In their flickering light the gold of the torc around Arthur's neck cut through the gloom, drew all our eyes to it.

I stayed near the entrance to the tent in the shadows, hoping no one would ask me to leave. The Council of Elders were there, all warriors or old men who were warlords once. Taran was among them, of course. I couldn't see his face, but his back was so stiff and straight, you could have used it as a table.

Where was Morcanta? They surely didn't forget to tell her! I smiled at that, imagining her fury.

Come to think of it, why had Morcanta allowed Arthur to take over the villa and move us all down here? I was deep in thought about that when something hit me sharply across the back.

'Ouch!'

I tried to turn but suddenly my head was wrapped tightly in thick cloth.

'Help! Arthur!'

I yelled with all my might but by now I was jolting along slung over someone's shoulder, my cries muffled. I started lashing out with my fists, hitting whoever it was but it was no good, I couldn't tell where to aim and my blows hardly connected. I was tossed onto the ground, the breath completely knocked out of me. The last thing I remember was a horrible cracking sound and a searing pain in the back of my head.

My Worst Fear

*It is too much. I will write about it later,
when I have time to lay my thoughts out
and look at them. Time, and heart.*

Someone was groaning. Where was I? Everything hurt. I opened my eyes and quickly clenched them shut again. A fire was hot on my face, making me see spots.

I groaned. I guess that was me groaning before. Felt so ill! I turned my head to the side and vomited. Lying on something cold and rough. I tried to move my hands. Bound! My legs too.

'Let her lie in her own vomit.'

I knew that voice. Tried to remember what had happened. I spit out the nasty slime in my mouth and tried not to gag.

'When will you inform Arthur?'

'I've sent Norwenna. She'll let him have one moment of glory, one moment of thinking he has outwitted me and become king. Then she'll tell him: his precious friend will die, unless he gives the torc to me! It is my right!'

I squinted my eyes slightly open and saw severed heads floating in the air above me. Then I realised it was just the faces of people standing over me, their faces lit up against the darkness. Morcanta's face was stark pale in the torchlight, her eyes blazing. She was mad, completely mad.

I groaned again.

'She wakes.'

'You will never be queen of Caerleon.' My mouth was too parched to do more than whisper, but she heard me.

'I will! This time, I will win!' She let the torch hover close to my face. I felt my hair singe and cried out. Morcanta laughed and moved the torch aside.

'Arthur will rescue me!'

'That's what I am counting on, *little sister* – a ransom! Your life in exchange for the torc and the kingdom. Or, if he refuses, I will offer you up to the gods. A life for a life! Your pathetic, miserable life, given in exchange for mine! I will rule, one way or another!'

Now I knew where I was. The altar stone in Druid Wood! I understood now why the stone had been cleared, who had used it to sacrifice an animal.

I tried to think what Arthur would do. He had the true torc; he should keep it. He was King Arthur now. No one would feel much loss at my death, or chide Arthur for choosing his kingdom over the life of one unimportant servant girl. My mother might, but I quickly put that thought from my mind.

Queen Aurelia said to pray. A lot of good that would do now! All we had worked for was at an end. Where did we go wrong? Wasn't it Arthur's destiny, to be king? It was what he was born to be. Why did this evil person have to snatch it out of his hands? What was God doing about it? In fact, where was he while all this was going on?

Let me do the thing in my own way. You do not always know what is best, Vibiana. Be patient and trust me. Wait – you will see what I will do!

Was that God speaking to me? It was like a voice I was hearing in my heart, but different from the anxious demanding voice of my own will. This was a gentle, kind knowing that just came into my mind from outside me. 'I will trust you,' I whispered through clenched teeth, so they wouldn't see my lips moving. 'Only help me – I don't know how!'

You are doing it now.

At that moment in spite of the aches in my body, the awful thought of Arthur giving up his kingdom – or of my own death! – I felt wrapped in a cloak, safe and warm. I felt God was smiling at me, but I didn't mind. It was the way you smile at a friend who's a bit foolish but you love them anyway.

I smiled too. Then I glanced at Morcanta. Her face was twisted with rage.

'This amuses you? I won't wait for Arthur! I'll cut out your heart and see if he can put it back again!' She drew a dagger from her belt and raised it over me. I saw the glint of a slender blade, held my breath for the coming blow. There was no time to pray but the thought flashed through my mind that I would be in Heaven before Zea. I smiled again and closed my eyes as the dagger lunged downward.

'Caradoc!'

The sound of Arthur's cry came at the same moment as a clatter and shriek of rage from Morcanta. My eyes flew open. Caradoc held both Morcanta's arms twisted tightly behind her, standing solid as a boulder in spite of her attempts to thrash about. I turned my head to see the dagger lying a hand's breadth from my face on the altar stone.

Several warriors with drawn swords surrounded Morcanta's women.

'Vibiana, are you hurt?'

I shook my head, which gave me a shooting pain. I guess I was hurt a little. Arthur used Morcanta's dagger to cut my bonds.

I noticed his neck was bare.

'Where is the torc?'

'You sound like a raven! But you're safe, that's the main thing.'

'Arthur, what have you done with the torc?' I had a feeling I knew.

'Magnus has it.'

The wise man stepped forward and held out the heavy ring. A necklace of golden strands, skilfully woven. The ruby eyes of the two dragon knobs sparkled in the torchlight.

Morcanta flinched as Magnus approached her.

'Let her go.'

Caradoc released Morcanta's arms slowly, watching for her to make a wrong move. Quick as a snake she snatched the torc greedily, secured it around her neck. In spite of its weight she held her head high.

'All my life I have known this was *my* destiny. I, Morcanta, the eldest child of Uther, have been chosen by the gods to rule all of Caerleon!'

'Hail, Morcanta!' shouted Norwenna, kneeling at her feet.

'Hail, Morcanta!' echoed the warrior women.

'No, Arthur!' This was foolish. 'I'm safe now; she can't hurt me. Keep the torc! You must be king, you must be!'

'Must I?'

I stared at him and tried to see the boy I played with, who called me Little Sister, but all I could see was a tall, blond youth, slender yet strong, who had suddenly become a man. Morcanta was already leading her women away.

Arthur shook his head sadly. 'This would never stop. Morcanta would never give up until she had the torc, the symbol of power.'

'She won't give it up now unless she's dead, and personally I'd like to help her along with that!'

'Think about it, Vibiana.' His voice held an echo of distant thunder. 'What is the kingdom worth, if I value it more than the life of my friend? I could have kept the torc, but I can't watch you every moment to protect you. Morcanta would have killed you soon to take revenge, and enjoyed doing it.'

I knew he was right, but everything was wrong!

'Let Morcanta rule the kingdom, if she can.' Arthur reached out to help me down from the altar stone.

'No! I won't go. I'm not worth it! Magnus, run quickly, get the torc back from Morcanta. Let her kill me, let her have her triumph but keep the kingdom safe!'

Arthur turned away and motioned to Caradoc. 'Come, all of you! We have a battle to fight, and someone must lead it.'

Before I knew what was happening I found myself slung over Caradoc's shoulder. For the second time that night I was carried like a sack of grain, taken against my will. I raged and sobbed until I had no strength left. Caradoc didn't say a word, just walked sturdily on until we were safely across the bridge and at the doorway of Julia's house.

Magnus had walked the whole way behind Caradoc, silent and withdrawn. As soon as Caradoc set me down, he put his hand on my arm.

'Vibiana.'

'What is it? Magnus, is it Zea?'

He nodded.

'I must go to her! I've been away too long – did the servant send for me?'

Magnus sighed.

'Vibiana –'

I banged on the door and flew inside the moment Julia opened. I knew from the look on her face. I knew, but I wouldn't believe it. My feet didn't want to obey me as I stumbled up the stairs to the rear chamber.

'Grandmother!' I called as I pushed aside the bed curtain.

Zea did not answer, as I knew she wouldn't. Several women stood there. They moved aside. I knelt by her bed and clasped her cold hand. It wasn't really that cold, not much more than when she was so ill the day of the flood. But I knew she was dead.

'She was old,' one of the women said gently. 'She lived a good, long life. It was her time.'

I nodded. I wanted to sob but I could not. I stared at the face of the one person who had loved me more than anyone else. It was peaceful. Maybe I imagined it, but I thought her mouth was turned ever so slightly upward in a smile.

The Second Ransom

A life for a life. I do not deserve it.
Not once but twice, someone paid
a ransom so that I could live.

We buried Zea in the tomb-house of the king's family, near the small chapel just behind the villa. Only a handful of us were there, come up from the safety of the town. It was cold but the rain had stopped and sun peeked through torn wisps of cloud.

She was laid to rest with prayers and a psalm chanted by the monks of Hibernia. Brendan sang a hymn he had invented just for her. I was glad to see the chi-ro, the symbol of Christ, carved on the stone sarcophagus which Magnus had had made months before. He had done what Zea would have wanted in spite of his own unbelief. He stood silently, his face a frozen mask of grief, as the rest of us sang and prayed.

Morcanta and her supporters had completely taken over the villa and moved the warriors and their gear in from the war-house. Every day she rode about on a silver grey horse with the torc on display around her neck, making sure everyone on both sides of the river knew she ruled Caerleon now.

Whenever I saw her coming, I hid. I'm ashamed to say it. I couldn't get over the fact that she'd almost killed me. I tried not to dwell on it, but sometimes in the lonely nights, with no Zea to look after, I pictured my own death in various scenes: my head severed, my heart cut out, my body reduced to a heap of ashes. There was nothing I could do except try to remember to pray. When I did, the scenes faded a little and I was usually able to sleep.

Arthur had told Morcanta he would keep Caliburn until after the invaders were vanquished. If they were. She agreed to this. I don't think she had skill with a sword and saw it as a symbol rather than something to use in battle.

Magnus stayed in the villa as well, with Gruffin, to keep an eye on his precious books and equipment. His greatest fear from the invaders was fire. Gruffin had been released from prison by the need of the moment, but his part in making the fake torc was still unclear.

Brendan joined me as we crossed the courtyard after the funeral, his harp under his arm. It looked like the town on market day, with dozens of makeshift open tents dotted around, where the warriors slept or ate or polished their equipment. The bathhouse cold room had been strewn with straw and made a perfect place to stable horses.

I had a lot to be grateful to Brendan for. He was the one who'd noticed me in the darkness of the campsite, slung over Norwenna's shoulder after they'd hit me on the head. He had followed us part way up the hill and then run back to get help.

'Any news of Bem?' I hadn't given him a thought until now, with everything else.

'None.'

'Have you looked for him?'

'Everywhere I can think of. Stinker has been with

me the whole time, he would have found Bem if he was there.'

'Have you tried looking up here, in the villa?'

'No one was allowed up here until today. Do you think—'

I looked for Arthur and saw him walking up ahead with Cai. No one noticed us.

'Come on!'

We turned aside and headed for Morcanta's quarters.

'Are you sure you can handle this?'

'Maybe you should ask if she can handle me!' I was tired of shrinking back every time I saw Morcanta.

'What do you want? My mistress is away.'

The woman with the pock-marked face blocked our way as we stepped under the veranda.

'We don't want her, Norwenna. You will do as well. We want to know where you're hiding Bem.'

When Norwenna smiled her hooked nose looked even sharper.

'There's no mystery about it. Would you like to see him?'

Brendan and I glanced at each other, mouths agape. I nodded.

Norwenna led us upstairs. She took a key from several hanging at her belt and unlocked a wooden door. We went inside and the door slammed and locked after us. The room had a close smell, making it hard to breathe. The thought crossed my mind that we were trapped, but she called out that she'd be back for us soon.

'Vibiana!'

At first I couldn't see because the small chamber was dark, with only one tiny window high in the wall.

'Bem!'

We hugged each other tightly, laughing and jumping up and down.

'What are you doing here?' Brendan asked.

'Lady. Sing for Lady.' Bem smiled and hummed a tune, nodding his head to its beat.

'But you're locked up! No one knew where you were! Come on, we have to get you out.'

I banged hard on the door and Norwenna unlocked it.

'It's time for you to go.'

'We're taking Bem with us!'

'Oh no, he stays here.' Norwenna shoved Bem back into the room and locked it before we could do anything.

'Why? He's harmless!'

'My mistress will let him go, when the time is right. She wants to keep him for now, just in case she needs him as ransom. I believe Arthur gave her the idea himself! It's well known how weak and soft-hearted he is.'

'And equally well known how hard-hearted your mistress is!'

'Come, Vibiana. It is no use, for now.'

I wanted to scratch Norwenna's poxy face but I knew Brendan was right. The whole villa was crawling with Morcanta's people. A rescue attempt would have been pointless. I let him drag me away. As we headed back down the narrow hallway I got a glimpse into one of the rooms through a half-closed curtain. I saw a table holding a small brazier and some kind of tools, and on the floor a bucket of something that looked very much like sand. So this was where the fake torc was made! I was careful to look straight ahead so Norwenna wouldn't notice what I'd seen.

Norwenna made sure we left and stood outside in the doorway watching us go. 'What will Arthur do,' she called after us, 'now that Taran and all his men support my mistress? Poor Arthur! He can join us, if he wants.'

'Gently, gently,' Brendan murmured in my ear. 'The Lord Christ has forgiven you; can you also forgive others?'

'I won't forgive Morcanta!' I kicked at a water barrel in my way and stubbed my toe.

Brendan said nothing, just hummed to himself and quietly plucked the harp. It was the tune he'd sung at Zea's funeral. My anger drained out of me and I walked silently beside him, a tear making its way down my cheek.

'Something I don't understand,' I said when he'd stopped playing.

'What is that?'

'Why did he do it?'

'Arthur, you mean. Give up his kingdom for you.'

'No. Well, that too! I mean, why should the Lord Christ forgive me? I really am a very bad person!'

By now we had reached the middle of the bridge across the Usk. We stopped and leaned our backs on the warm stone. Brendan grinned at me, his grey eyes sparkling like the winter sun on the water.

'Yes, that is it!'

'What is?'

'The whole story. The question, and the answer. Why would anyone give up his kingdom, his life, for a bad person like you?'

'Don't tease me! I am bad, I'm not just saying that!'

'No, I do not mean to tease. I am bad as well.'

'No you aren't! I'm bossy, I know I am. Mostly I think only of myself. I can't even love my mother as I should. And I certainly don't love Morcanta! But look at you: dressed up like a monk, travelling half-way around the world in a leaky boat, spending hours in prayer every day, all because you believe in the Lord Christ. Because he is your *friend*, as you told me once.'

I moved on and Brendan followed. Arthur would be at the theatre, and I wanted to tell him about Bem, and about what I had seen in Morcanta's quarters.

'That does not make me good, not here.' Brendan tapped his chest. 'The only thing that can make me good, is the Lord's sacrifice. His death, in exchange for my bad life.'

'The ransom.'

'What is this word, ransom?'

'Just what you said. A price paid, to set someone free, like Arthur paid the price of the torc and his kingdom, so that I could live.'

'Yes! You understand it now.'

'Not exactly. I still have many questions.'

The sound of hoofbeats on the bridge behind us made me turn.

'Look – there's Taran!'

Brendan and I moved aside to let the tall black horse pass by. Taran tugged on the reins as he neared us. He halted so close to me, I felt the horse's soft breath on my face.

'You are a friend of Arthur.'

I nodded. What could he want? I tried to summon up a feisty retort but nothing came to mind as I stared up at him.

'Tell me where he camps.'

'In the old amphitheatre. His tent is the large one there.'

Taran nodded and spun his mount around with a speed that had Brendan and me leaping backwards for safety. He trotted back across the bridge then as he reached the other side, turned east and kicked the sleek black into a full gallop. Within three blinks of an eye he was up the hill and out of sight.

'Why did he go back if he wants to find Arthur?'

'Who knows? We'd better tell Arthur right away!'

As we made our way hastily down to the old Roman theatre, I thought how odd it all was. Arthur had paid the ransom and sacrificed his kingdom, and doing that seemed to make him into a real king, except now he couldn't be, because he had given up his right to rule. Where would it end?

The Battle for Caerleon

I hope I only wounded with my arrows,
that my victims were among the living
when the battle ended. I do not know.

The night was bitterly cold, with damp mist rising out of the river below. Although there were hundreds of us, we crouched quietly on the wet grass on both sides of the High Hill above the villa, showing no light to betray our presence.

Hundreds of us, yet thousands of them, it seemed! The invaders camped on the hillside below, between us and the villa, careless of their fires and noise. They thought we were still inside the villa, knew we were outnumbered and reckoned on us giving way like a feeble bunch of old women. They would be surprised!

'Please, God!' I said under my breath.

After midnight our people had crossed the bridge and fanned out a distance along the river, then turned uphill. Now, while the barbarians supposed they had us surrounded on three sides, in fact we surrounded them!

Arthur and Cai were on horseback, and I knew Taran and Caradoc were as well, somewhere in the line on the hill, though I couldn't see them. Cai held a shuttered lantern, its small flame no danger to us. In spite of the cold, sweat dripped down from under Arthur's pointed metal helmet, soaking his face.

'If only it doesn't rain.' Cai's face was striped with light and shadow.

Arthur nodded. 'Even the mist will dampen our torches before we light them. Tell the people to cover them in their cloaks, for now.' Cai began to give the orders, which were passed in both directions along the lines.

I left them and picked my way among the people of Caerleon, everyone old enough to stay up this late. Many carried small containers of glowing charcoal, to light the torches. Each was ready with clay pots and iron knives, or whatever piece of metal they could find. I smiled at that, wondering what the enemy would make of us if they could see an army of all ages, decked out with cooking gear!

'That Arthur, he's that clever!' I heard an old man whisper as I walked past.

'Too clever for me,' said a woman. 'I don't see what my slop bucket has to do with it!'

'I get to blow a trumpet, do you want to hear it?' a child asked.

'Shh!' someone else said. 'Not until we're told.'

Further down the hill the chariots were spread out in a long line. In each chariot the driver sat with an unlit flare lashed upright beside him, and a warrior with bow and arrows or spear standing behind. Even though the chariot beds were cleverly designed to hang on a frame to smooth the ride, still each warrior was lashed to the sides by a rope at his waist. The lightweight wagons pulled by two ponies would bump downhill at a great pace, and the men needed both hands free for battle. Not only men, for I would be riding a chariot as well.

The archers were quietly flexing their bows, pulling on the strings and releasing them. That sent twanging sounds echoing down the hillside, and I walked along the line, putting my finger to my lips in warning. Some of the men smiled at me, some glared, others pretended not to see me. But all ceased their noise, that was the main thing.

As I walked along, I remembered Zea telling Arthur and me the story of Gideon, and how he defeated a great army with only a few men. As if carried back, I saw us in the flecked shade under the apple tree, Zea small and fragile in her wheelchair, yet smiling so joyfully.

'God, why did she have to die?'

Without warning I began to sob. I moved quickly away from the line of warriors, ran down the hill and threw myself to the ground at the foot of a tree. I huddled there for an age, letting the hot tears flow. 'Why?' I asked over and over again. 'Why?' I knew all the reasons: she was old, she'd had a good life, it was her time and all of that – but it wasn't enough!

When all my tears were spent I sat there, my head buried in my knees, waiting for God to chide me. Oddly, it seemed to me that he didn't. Gradually I felt the tide of a strange calm and peace rising in my heart, until it was full. I had no answer to my questions but felt my heart eased of them, at least for now.

I wiped my face on my tunic and went to find my chariot. It stood at the west end of the line, my charioteer waiting, my own curved yew bow ready for me. Arthur hadn't wanted me to join the battle, but I persuaded him. 'If I'm on the end, we can veer off at any sign of real danger. You know I'm one of the best archers.' He'd stared hard at me and finally shrugged. I guess he thought I'd figure a way to join in somehow, and he'd rather know what I was up to!

Thinking of that reminded me, we didn't know what Morcanta was up to. Surely she and her women wouldn't stay in her chamber at the villa, while the rest of us fought the barbarians!

The most amazing thing had happened. Taran had come secretly to Arthur's tent three nights before. He'd stayed talking until first light and by the end of it, Taran had pledged his allegiance to Arthur. Cai told me he said he'd rather fight under the command of a boy, than be muck under the heel of an ignorant woman. Cai thought Taran was impressed in spite of himself, when he heard what Arthur wanted to do. The next night he'd managed to get all of his men and their horses and arms out of the villa and over the river before Morcanta realised what was happening.

There was always the chance Morcanta would try to take revenge on Arthur in the midst of the battle. Arthur had informed her of his plan to strike, hoping for her help, but she refused. It was not for him to plan, she said, but for her as queen. But she wouldn't reveal her mind. She still had about a third of the warriors, those who were not strong supporters either of Arthur or Taran. But I knew Magnus was in the villa, guarding his quarters. If she tried anything against us, he'd send us word by Gruffin.

It was nearing the darkest hour. As soon as the invaders slept, we would strike. I peered anxiously into the gloom but there was no moon. I could see nothing except the faint flicker of oil lamps in some of the villa windows, lit by Magnus and Gruffin to deceive the invaders.

I ran back to where my chariot waited and climbed aboard. I struggled to pull on the slippery vest of ring mail and jammed my helmet on my head. Immediately I felt trickles of sweat running down beside my ears.

'I'll tie you in.'

I stood with feet firmly planted while the charioteer quickly secured the rope around my waist and then to one side of the frame, showing me exactly how to release it if I needed to get free in a hurry. He was old but seemed to know his art.

'Brace yourself against my back once we start. Be sure you pull that and jump clear if we start to go over. Otherwise you'll be trapped underneath, dragged to your death, most likely.'

'Don't worry, I understand.'

I took several deep breaths, bent my bow and very nearly released it until I remembered to do it slowly so it wouldn't make noise. I made sure all my arrows were in my quiver and in good position for grabbing with one hand, then slung and fixed it securely across my back.

I practised silently. Arrow – set – pull – release! The main thing was to get into a good rhythm. I would do it without thinking but now to calm myself I repeated the sequence in my mind, going over and over it until I was ready to scream with impatience. For a long time now there had been no noise and few lights from the barbarians below us. Why didn't we start?

Suddenly the night was pierced by the high clear call of a lone trumpet.

The next moment the whole hillside shook with the din. Trumpets blared, clay pots shattered, torches flared alight. With a tremendous roar as if from the throat of a giant dragon, the people of Caerleon attacked.

A few moments later by our torchlight I glimpsed invaders racing out of their tents fully armed, but we were already on the move. What a sight that must have been! I could just imagine the barbarians hearing crashes as if the earth split open, running out to see winged chariots of fire swarming down the hillside. They must have thought it was the judgement of their gods!

Their leaders ran for the few horses while the rest defended themselves on foot. I saw the chieftain, knew him because he was broad and sturdy as an oak door. He swung onto his tall horse carrying battle axe and spear in one hand and shield in the other. A long sword hung at his side and a shorter one was stuck through his belt.

'The Lord protect King Arthur and his kingdom!'

'Amen!' This heartfelt shout from the charioteer made me realise I'd spoken aloud.

We jolted down the hill. I steadied my legs against the driver's bony back and set an arrow at the ready. Behind us I heard the blare of trumpets and shouts of the people of Caerleon, the clatter of knives on metal dishes and continual smashing of pots. A small breeze blew up and the mist cleared, letting a bit of moonlight onto the scene.

Our chariots reached the barbarian camp!

Every man of theirs carried a spear, many had axes and swords as well. If they couldn't hit one of us they could hack at the horses, overturn the chariots.

Pull – release! My arrow sank straight into a barbarian's arm, just as he'd raised his spear. I only wounded him, he was down and up again in a flash but now out of my sight. We drove on at wind-speed, coming close and then circling around to stay out of the enemy's reach, then back in again.

'Well done!' I called to my driver, who seemed to turn the ponies in mid-air to twist us out of the way of a well-thrown spear. I pulled and shot, hitting the spearman in the chest. He was down.

I shot my arrows again and again, using all in my shoulder quiver and from the four spare quivers at my feet. Some wore chain mail under their tunics and the arrows bounced off. I had many good hits and may have killed a few men. I hope I didn't but at the time I did what had to be done and didn't think about it. Arthur had said to spare women and children even though the Council was fully against that. So he said, kill only those who attack, spare the others.

It didn't go for us as it did for Gideon in the story. Instead of running away in fear, the barbarians stood their ground and fought like madmen.

Where was Morcanta? She must have seen from her rear windows what was happening. We could have used her help! I hadn't reckoned on her being a coward.

Nor was she.

It happened at the height of the battle.

Most of us were fighting our own little battles, trying to wound and keep from being wounded. Out of the corner of my eye I saw Arthur fall from his horse.

'That way!' I shouted.

The chariot veered, bumped over several bodies.

By the time I neared him he was on his feet, Caliburn in one hand and shield in the other. Then I saw the barbarian chieftain only ten paces away. He was mounted, still holding his axe, its blade dripping gore. The huge man hesitated for one eye-blink then leaped to the ground, tossing his axe to one side and drawing his sword. Like Caliburn it was long and double-bladed.

Tensed for attack, the bearded invader stared Arthur right in the eye, and Arthur stared back. It was almost as if they could read each other's thoughts! I couldn't believe my eyes when they each threw aside their shields, clasped both hands on their swords and lifted them in the air.

'For Caerleon!' Arthur yelled.

The barbarian shouted something, and they lunged forward. All this time I was not calmly watching but shooting arrows as fast as I could, my charioteer guiding the horse in and out but always in sight of these two. I knew Arthur wouldn't thank me for aiming at the chieftain, so I simply tried to keep a clear field for them and others nearby did the same. The swords sliced the air and struck, sending up sparks. They leaped back, then swirled their swords again, brought the sharp blades whistling down in a deadly arc. Again, Caliburn stuck the barbarian's sword, but not his body.

'Arthur! Arthur!'

I think we were all yelling now, I don't know, my ears were ringing and I was hot and sweaty, dimly aware that Arthur was smaller, younger, weaker than this giant of a man. Yet it didn't seem so. He had the strength of a dozen. Arthur lifted Caliburn once more, brought the blade in a sideways arc while jumping like a hare. The opponent's sword missed but Caliburn connected, striking the barbarian's ribs.

The clang of metal told me the invader wore ring mail under his tunic, but the blow knocked him off balance and he staggered, almost dropping his sword. In that moment Arthur pressed his advantage and struck again, this time slicing at his thigh. There wasn't time to lift Caliburn up to aim for the neck.

'He's down!'

The charioteer shouted over his shoulder as we whirled around and galloped back up the hill.

'Wait!' I called.

The chariot turned and halted, clear of the fighting. Morcanta had appeared suddenly from around the eastern side of the villa, flanked by armed and mounted women, warriors following them. She rode the silver grey. The flicker of torches and the shreds of moonlight showed the gleam of gold at her neck.

She carried a spear and raised it now in a fierce gesture. I wondered if she knew how to use it.

'People of Caerleon! Your queen will save you from the enemy! Follow my lead!'

There was a moment of stunned silence in the midst of the battle. The invaders had no idea who she was, and the rest of us just couldn't believe her stupidity.

In a funny way she did save Caerleon. The fallen barbarian chieftain sprang to his feet with a roar, blood pouring from his thigh. With incredible strength he ran towards Morcanta and leaped up behind her on the grey. Before I could catch my breath he had kicked the horse and ridden off eastward. Morcanta dropped her spear and struggled in vain. With one powerful hand the barbarian gripped the reins and Morcanta; with the other he wrenched the gold torc from her neck. The last thing I saw was the broad back of the barbarian as he rode away, the torc held high in triumph.

The rest of the invaders fled, killing as they ran. I saw Norwenna go down with a spear in her chest and felt a pang of regret that I had hated her. Some barbarian women and children remained in their campsite, huddled together waiting for death. They were spared along with the wounded, but would have to live with us now and make the best of it.

A slender figure dashed at me out of the darkness.

'God be praised! I was looking all over for you. You are safe!'

It was over. We had won. As I stood clinging tightly to Llian I felt a surge of excitement at our victory, dampened by the sickening knowledge that we had taken life that God had given.

Arthur! Arthur! Arthur!

I could almost hear the roar of the crowds, the snarling of wild beasts, the terrified cries of prisoners. The old theatre was put to better use today.

Hundreds sat on the grassy banks surrounding the arena, where years ago gladiators fought and prisoners died to entertain the masses. Today, the people of Caerleon gathered to see their king for the first time in the light of day.

'My people!' Arthur lifted his hands, and the crowd leaped to their feet, cheering and whistling. He stood on a large flat stone in the centre of the grassy theatre, flanked by Cai and his five chief warriors.

Taran was one of the five. He looked completely at ease with being under Arthur's rule, but I couldn't help wondering how far he could be trusted.

A light snow had fallen in the night, making scrunching sounds under our feet, but now the sky was blue. The banks of the theatre provided shelter from the wind and the sun beat down, blinding where it glanced off spears and helmets of the warriors.

Arthur was bare-headed, unarmed except for Caliburn sheathed, hanging from his sword-belt. His purple cloak was caught at the shoulder with a heavy golden brooch. The wind whipped it back and I saw with relief that someone had persuaded him to wear new trousers and a tunic edged with embroidery.

His mother, probably. She sat tall and straight in her carved chair on the edge of the grass. Underneath her dignified air I could sense her delight and pride. She wore no jewellery, and now I knew why. Norwenna had stolen the queen's heavy gold necklace, fashioned it into the torc for Morcanta to wear at the feast. So although it was a fake, it was solid gold. It was part of the king's treasure but Arthur said he didn't want to wear it.

Arthur waved again and the crowd went wild.

'Ar-thur, Ar-thur, Ar-thur!'

The monks and nuns were a blob of brown in the crowd to my left. They were shouting right along with the rest. I saw one mop of curly dark hair among the shaved high foreheads, and waved. I didn't know if Brendan saw me or not.

A shaggy brown dog wove in and out of people seated on the snowy grass, following right on the heels of Bem. I was so glad he was finally safe!

The chant grew and swelled until it seemed the river and hills and trees must have joined in. With Taran's support and Morcanta gone, there was no doubt that this ruler was the one they would follow.

Arthur grinned like a boy. I saw him glance around quickly from side to side and he frowned slightly but then smiled again and kept on waving until the people finally grew quiet. I had been searching the crowd, wondering where Magnus could possibly be. It seemed wrong that he was not at Arthur's side. I hoped no one would think Arthur didn't have his full support.

The chanting died down and there was a moment of silence. We were all wondering what would happen next, for Arthur had said all the people were to gather but didn't tell why.

In the quiet came a sound, the slow creaking of a cart.

The crowd on the side near the river parted. Magnus walked into the ring, leading a pony which pulled a small cart filled with straw. Gruffin rode in the cart, his arms spread wide to hold a large round object. He had been cleared of any wrong in the making of the fake torc, saying Morcanta forced him to admit blame. Apparently Norwenna had made sure to use sand from Magnus' workroom, to put suspicion on Gruffin. With Norwenna dead and Morcanta gone, we would never know for sure.

'Oohh!'

The crowd spoke as one, when they saw the globe of green glass resting on the straw. It looked like a gigantic glass eye, reflecting the sun.

Magnus led the pony into the centre and joined Arthur on the stone. He held up his hand for silence.

'We the people are Caerleon are grateful to God for victory over the barbarians –'

A huge cheer broke out and Magnus waited for it to die down.

'–and for giving us a new king!'

'Ar-thur, Ar-thur!'

Again Magnus waited. I couldn't help thinking of King Uther, almost forgotten by us all, on his deathbed in Julia's house. In view of the dangerous times, the Council had decided to let Arthur take over even though his father still clung to life. I hoped Uther had been able to understand that his son was king. Maybe someone would have opened the shutters of his window, so he could hear the crowd and feel glad his kingdom was secure.

Magnus spoke. 'Through the years, our people have worshipped many gods: those of the Romans, the gods of trees and rivers, strange gods from the East. Life moves on, yet we cling to the old gods.'

He lifted his shoulders and pursed his lips, causing the creases of his face to stand out sharply in the sunlight and shadow.

'I was guilty of this. I thought we could make use of any gods, as we needed them. I understand more clearly now, there is only one God of light. If we open ourselves to the others, we take darkness into ourselves.

'I have done that, but now, in front of you all, I renounce the old gods. I will worship the Lord Christ, and Him alone.'

That was what Zea meant! Until this moment I had completely forgotten her last words to me: 'You must be one or the other, not both.' I had thought she was babbling, but she was trying to warn Magnus. I realised he had come to the same understanding on his own.

As I had. I was heartily sorry I had ever had even a small part in encouraging Magnus in his dark arts. If those in Heaven could see what happened on earth, Zea was smiling right now!

Magnus stepped down from the stone and motioned for the warriors to help him. Between them they lifted the globe from the cart, took straw from the cart and placed it on the flat stone, then lowered the globe until it rested securely on a bed of straw atop the stone.

'Move back, and cover your faces!'

Caradoc handed Magnus an axe. The warriors and Arthur pulled their cloaks in front of their faces. With one elbow Magnus crooked his cloak up to protect himself, and with the other arm he raised the axe high. I could make out swirls in the surface of the glass, curling shapes that seemed to beckon me to look closer. It was a pity to destroy something so beautiful. We might need the globe to tell us what to expect in the future, to help us prepare for another attack. I wanted to argue, urge Magnus to think again.

'In the name of Christ!' Magnus called out as he struck with all his might.

There was a crash as of a thousand glass jars shattering and a sudden smell of something rotten, which quickly disappeared. I felt dizzy. I shook my head, blinked, and looked again at the glass globe. All that was left of it were shards scattered all over the straw and for a great distance around. People were carefully picking pieces of it out of their hair or clothing. The shards were not green but a dull, dirty black.

There was a long low letting go of breath, like wind in the treetops. Then people began leaving the ampitheatre, first only a few, then more and more until it was like a stampede with everyone trying to get away at once. It was a cheerful, polite stampede though, with lots of shouted apologies as toes were trodden on. Arthur looked as puzzled as I felt. Magnus merely smiled. He must have guessed right away what was happening.

Before long, those who were first to leave had returned, struggling through to the centre with their arms full. I shouldered my way down so I could be close enough to hear.

'We don't really worship them you understand, it's just a bit of decoration for the living room.' A mother pressed her children forward; they carried several small clay household gods, the kind that would sit in a niche at home and hopefully bring good fortune.

'Thank you. Place them here.' Magnus pointed to the bed of straw, and the children set down the clay figures.

'This was handed down by my great-grandfather and I didn't like to throw it away.' An elderly man held out a bronze statue of the god Mercury, wings sprouting from its ankles and head. As the day wore on, every household in Caerleon gave up its old gods, placed them on the growing pile on the stone.

At one point Magnus said in a low voice, for my ears alone, 'I never understood it.'

'What?'

'The point of it, a life for a life. I saw it that night, when Arthur laid aside his kingdom to save you. It was not weakness, but great strength.'

'It looked like weakness! It was foolish, even though it turned out well.'

'Yes. Love is most strong when it is willing to appear weak.'

That was something I would have to think about, but it rang true. Darkness was falling already. I had forgotten— it was nearing the shortest day. A cheer went up as fire was laid to the pile, which had been doused with oil. The light blazed up, banishing the gloom.

'We will worship the one true God!'

Someone started the chant and it grew as the flames leaped higher, lighting up the deep blue sky. I joined in and yelled until I was hoarse.

Arthur grinned at me as we moved well back from the crackling blaze. Every so often there was a loud *bang* as a piece of clay exploded.

'You made it. You're really the king – King Arthur!'

'I know. What now?'

'You rule. You lead the people, win many battles, die an old man surrounded by your grandchildren.'

'All right, Vibiana, I'll take your advice.'

Arthur tapped me playfully on the shoulder and moved off to speak to someone else. I noticed he didn't call me Little Sister. That was as it should be. We couldn't stay children forever. It was time to move on.

Setting Sail

'What happens next?'

Whenever Brendan tells a story, if he stops in the middle the children sitting at his feet tug at his tunic and demand to hear the rest.

For myself, that's what I always want to know as well. This is what happened next for us, the people of Caerleon.

Half a year has gone by and the longest day approaches. Brendan sits on the bench under the largest apple tree each evening after dinner, singing songs, telling tales and legends or stories out of the Scriptures. By now he speaks our language like one of us and knows how to change his voice, making it high and squeaky or low and fierce, according to each character.

The villa children will sit hardly breathing for as long as he talks, until their parents come and carry them off to bed, while they call out for 'just one more'. Some of them don't have parents; they are barbarian children left behind in the raid. Our people have taken them in, though some still look lost and sad. When these ones come for evening stories they always huddle around Bem, sucking their thumbs or stroking Stinker. They don't even seem to notice the smell.

The one story the children always ask for is Gideon, because you can't tell of Gideon and not tell the whole tale of that awful night when barbarians almost took over Caerleon, when they did take away Morcanta and the torc, when King Arthur saved us by his strength and cunning. Brendan is careful to say these two stories, of Gideon and of Arthur, really happened, so they begin to learn the difference between truth and make-believe.

I am too busy to keep my record-book these days. I have a very important job. Magnus has appointed me Chief Librarian, or so he calls it. The old bath room which was then a stables, has now become library and scriptorium. I have seven of Feoras' monks in my charge. Our task is to list, repair and copy every scroll or book in Magnus' collection. It is hard work but I love it. Two of the monks assist me in the cleaning and careful recording of our treasures – for the written word is as valuable as gold – and five monks spend all their days at special wooden desks, copying the texts. When a book is important, they will paint beautiful pictures or patterns in the margins, though there isn't much time for that.

Feoras and the other monks will take some of the copies with them when they leave us, which will be soon, before the autumn storms. That way, the wisdom and learning which Magnus preserved in his locked cupboards, will spread across the world along with the Gospel of Christ.

Except for one book of wisdom. We still have it, the book of ancient magic. Magnus is the only one who can read it, and in any case, he has no use for it. He says, why bother with magic when you can know the God who created the universe? The old arts are weak by comparison. I think he looks younger now, as if a few of the lines on his face have disappeared.

The dining room has become a school when not used for meals. Five monks join Feoras there every day to teach the people, as many of the villa and town who will come. Most cannot read but they have learned the Scriptures by heart. Feoras makes sure they also know not just the words, but what they mean, how to live their lives in the ways of Christ.

Magnus often sits at the back of the room, listening quietly. I notice he and Feoras have begun taking long walks together, and that Feoras seems to do most of the talking.

'Vibiana! You will miss dinner if you do not come at once! Your books will wait for you.'

'Coming!'

That is Llian – my mother. She and the others from the Abbey all moved to buildings within the villa walls. Other invaders will come someday, and the High Hill is safe no longer. Queen Aurelia joined the Abbey after the death of King Uther, and now spends her days quietly in prayer or simple tasks.

Llian stops by to see me every day. She's becoming a bit bossy and I do get irritated with her sometimes – just the way you do with a real mother! I'm not complaining, though. I know what it's like not to have a mother. So my heart is glad we're together, even though we have a lot to learn about getting along.

We have heard no news of Morcanta, but sometimes I think of her in idle moments, try to imagine her fate. Some say the chieftain would take her as wife, but I can never picture her as the servile wife of a barbarian. I am sure, if she lives, she is making someone's life a misery! The torc went with her but Arthur doesn't need it in order to rule, for his kingship depends on his courage and kindness, not on a piece of gold.

He is having another torc fashioned for himself, from some of the torcs and bracelets we found in the Druid's pond. Bem led us to the spot deep in the undergrowth where our ancestors left them. Magnus thinks they were thrown there not only as an offering to the gods but also to hide them from the conquering Romans.

As for Arthur, he is already loved by the people for bringing peace and safety to the kingdom. Magnus assures me the tests to his character have hardly begun, that it remains to be seen if his soft heart will be a stumbling block when it is time to unite all of Britain against the invading hordes. Nonetheless, he has Magnus to advise him, Cai to spur him on and my prayers to follow him on all his adventures.

When the monks sail south, my work with the library will be done. Then I will leave as well, and Llian with me. Brendan has invited a few of us to visit his home in the west of Hibernia, the country he calls Erin, to meet his parents and his six brothers and sisters and to see his pigs! He's begun teaching us their language, to make us ready.

Brendan thinks the life of a monk is not for him, and I agree.

When he told me this, I felt a happiness deep inside and I might have blushed, but he didn't notice.

Who knows what the future will hold for us? No one can see it, not really, even with a magic glass globe. Only God knows it inside out, the end from the beginning and from side to side. Zea might have said something like that.

I smile at the thought, and follow Llian across the courtyard to join my friends.

Ten Things to know about

1 Who was the real King Arthur?

He was probably a strong warlord who lived about a hundred years after the Romans left Britain. Romantic stories of knights of the Round Table, Guinevere and Lancelot were invented much later. The real Arthur would likely have been a British Celt who followed the Christian faith and Roman customs. His name is connected with a decisive victory over the invading Anglo-Saxons in about 516 AD. Arthur is often symbolised by a red dragon. The dragon image was probably brought to Wales by the Romans and is found on the Welsh national flag today.

2 Where was King Arthur's court?

'Camelot' where Arthur ruled is claimed by many places including Glastonbury in Somerset, Caerleon in South Wales and Tintagel in

Cornwall. There is little real evidence, although excavations at Tintagel turned up a sixth-century slate reading 'Artognou had this made'. The 'kingdom of Caerleon' and the king's villa in the story are imaginary. The Roman Second Legion was stationed at Caerleon and the amphitheatre and other ruins are worth a visit.

3 Where did Celts keep their treasure?

Often it was in the form of gold or silver jewellery, which could be buried in the ground for safekeeping. The Celts were iron-age peoples who occupied the British Isles before the Romans came. They were great warriors, often going naked into battle except for a heavy neck-ring called a torc. They frightened their enemies with painted bodies and hair stiffened with lime to make it stand out wildly. The British Museum has a collection of torcs in its Romano-British exhibit.

4 Why was the Celtic chariot superior?

It had wheels rimmed with iron and a light-weight platform suspended from wooden frame. Their charioteers were expert drivers, astonishing the invading Romans with their skill in handling the two ponies. Each chariot carried a warrior with spear or slingshot, plus the driver. Sometimes dead warriors would be buried in their chariots.

5 Why were the Druids important?

Druids were ancient pagan priests, who were in charge of Celtic culture, scholarship and law. They even had authority over the tribal chiefs. Druids worshipped at nature shrines in sacred groves and studied the stars and planets. They

believed in the sacrifice of one life to save another— that an unimportant person could be sacrificed to save someone more valuable.

6 What did the Romans leave behind?

Central hypocaust heating, hot baths, good highways, aqueducts and amphitheatres - these can still be seen today. The Romans were excellent engineers and soldiers, spreading their influence all over the modern continent of Europe. They also gave us Latin, the foundation of the modern 'Romance' languages. Because they kept good written records, most of what we know about the Celts comes from Roman writings.

7 What was life like in Britain after the Romans?

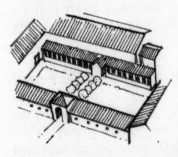

After the fall of Rome in the fifth century AD, many native Britons continued to live in large country estates known as 'villas' such as Chedworth in Gloucestershire. Instead of being ruled by Rome, the people were led by whatever tribal chiefs could take control. In areas such as Wroxeter the stones of Roman buildings were carted away to make dwellings for the Britons. Trade and civilisation began to decline.

8   How did the Irish bring light to the Dark Ages?

While Germanic tribes were sweeping across Europe and Britain, destroying centuries of learning, Christian monks in Ireland were quietly copying not only the Scriptures but also the great classical writings.   Starting in the early sixth century AD, missionaries from Ireland began to spread the gospel throughout the known world.   They also brought with them the classics that had been lost or destroyed, eventually causing libraries to spring up again.

9   What was Christianity like in the Dark Ages?

Emperor Constantine had made Christianity the official religion of the Roman empire in the late fourth century AD. Some people kept their old pagan worship alongside the newer Christian faith. There were two main kinds of

 Christian worship, Roman and Celtic. The Celtic monks from Ireland practised a strict tradition of prayer and fasting, living as simply as possible. The Roman tradition was more relaxed: monks had two cooked meals a day, wine, and a mattress and pillow to sleep on. In the seventh century AD a meeting of both groups decided in Rome's favour.

10 Who ruled Britain after Arthur?

Tribes of Angles, Saxons, Friesians and Jutes invaded southern and eastern Britain= in the fifth and sixth century AD. They were part of the Germanic tribes who moved westward and took over as the Roman Empire weakened. They are known as 'Anglo-Saxons'  and it was their language that was the basis for English. They created small farming or fishing communities rather than towns and were excellent craft workers.

If you enjoyed this book
look out for our other title
in the series

TALES · OUT · OF · TIME

CORIN'S
Quest
DONNA VANN

Time Period: Middle Ages

Torchbearers
Danger On The Hill
by C. Mackenzie

"Run, run for your lives," a young boy screamed. "Run, everybody, run. The soldiers are here."

That day on the hill is the beginning of a new and terrifying life for the three Wilson children. Margaret, Agnes and Thomas are not afraid to stand up for what they believe in, but it means that they are forced to leave their home and their parents for a life of hiding on the hills.

If you were a covenanter in the 1600s you were the enemy of the King and the authorities. But all you really wanted to do was worship God in the way he told you to in the Bible. Margaret wants to give Jesus Christ the most important place in her life, and this conviction might cost her life.

There is danger on the hill for Margaret. There is danger everywhere - if you are a covenanter.

The Torchbearers series are true life stories from history where Christians have suffered and died for their faith in Christ.

ISBN 1 85792 7842

CHRISTIAN FOCUS

Staying faithful – Reaching out!

Christian Focus Publications publishes books for adults and children under its three main imprints: Christian Focus, Mentor and Christian Heritage. Our books reflect that God's word is reliable and Jesus is the way to know him, and live forever with him.

Our children's publication list includes a Sunday school curriculum that covers pre-school to early teens; puzzle and activity books. We also publish personal and family devotional titles, biographies and inspirational stories that children will love.

If you are looking for quality Bible teaching for children then we have an excellent range of Bible story and age specific theological books.

From pre-school to teenage fiction, we have it covered!

Find us at our web page:
www.christianfocus.com